A DYING ART

ALSO BY AARON HILTON
Skin Deep Motives
Can't Beat a Classic
The Grunge Operatives

A DYING ART

A NOVELLA

AARON HILTON

PORTLAND, OREGON

A BACKWATER CRIME BOOK

First Paperback Edition: December 2017

Copyright © 2017 by Aaron Hilton

Edited by Ariel Hudnall
Cover Design by Aaron Hilton
Featuring Brianna LeBlanc as Emma Rooney
Makeup & F/X by Crystal Laird
Author Photograph by Angelique Herrington
Featuring Melissa Kate as The Muse
Backwater Crime logo & Gunman Silhouette by
Daniel Cooney

This story is a work of fiction. Names, characters, places and incidents are products of the writer's imagination and used fictitiously. Any resemblance to actual events, locales, or persons living or dead is totally coincidental.

ISBN 978-0-9853941-6-5

This is for my mom, Charlotte Lee-Shea.
Deeply missed.
She raised survivors.

AUTHOR'S NOTE

Although *A Dying Art* doesn't feature the Grunge Operatives of Alternative Investigations, this story introduces supporting characters integral to the series moving forward.

Aaron Hilton

October, 2017

A DYING ART

PROLOGUE

October, 2000

The teenage girl stumbled out of the tree line. Dead leaves clung to her knotted black hair. The skin of her upper arms and thighs bore scratches from Douglas Fir needles, and claw marks from where the bastards had held her down. An owl perched on a branch nearby hooted. The wavering sound startled her. As her bare feet negotiated the steep, uneven terrain, she slipped on a patch of sodden mulch. Tumbling forward, she struck a ditch.

Emma Rooney's face crunched against bedrock. The impact broke her nose; surprisingly enough, it hadn't been during the assault earlier. Emma stiffened her split, swollen lips, and pushed herself up. A fresh stream of blood ran into her mouth. A worm squeezed through her fingers as she clutched a handful of moist earth.

Standing up on heavy, wobbly legs, Emma stepped onto asphalt. She focused on following the white line and reflectors. She took comfort in leaving behind the tree frogs croaking in the woods for the vehicles zooming past her on the interstate.

A gust of wind knocked her off balance. Emma waved her arms to compensate. A Mercedes Benz sped along, a guy standing up through the sunroof. He howled at the moon, a fifth of booze in his fist.

"Nice tits!" he yelled.

Overcome with shame and shock, Emma covered up her nude breasts with her arms. She started to walk. It was more of a hobble.

She didn't know how many miles she covered. All she focused on was trying to breathe through blood-clotted nostrils and making distance.

A road sign up ahead indicated Portland was twenty miles north. She shivered and moved on. Her teeth chattered. Just a few feet past the sign, a gut-wrenching abdominal pain forced her over. The pressure reminded her of a kickoff, only her stomach and her uterus were the football. She fell down; jagged gravel scraped up her kneecaps.

The scream that exploded through her lips was covered up by a log truck. She gagged and retched. The few bites of chicken salad she'd consumed at the homecoming tailgate party resembled moldy cream of mushroom soup.

Her nerves acclimated to the pain. Gritting her teeth, she stood back up. Pressing a hand to her stomach, she noticed that her pink cotton panties were now soiled through with blood, dirt, and sweat. Despite feeling dizzy, Emma began to move again.

Raindrops started to spit. The dark gray shroud of clouds coughed a set of rolling booms before dumping sheets of rain. The thick droplets streamed down Emma's ravaged body. The water washed away the blood on her black and blue thighs. She wept.

Looking down at her feet, Emma continued to follow the white line. Rainwater coursing down the incline distorted the safety zone beneath ripples. She didn't realize that she'd walked out into the highway until a horn blared.

Spinning around, Emma screamed for the car to stop, then threw her arms up to her bruised and battered face. The pickup swerved around, splashing her with water that tasted of motor oil. She smelled burnt rubber. She backpedaled, terrified.

The massive lights of a semi truck were climbing up the hill toward her. Its horn blared. The whining of the air breaks caused Emma's legs to shake, before she froze in the drenching coldness.

The rig shuddered to a halt. Squinting through the rain dripping from her soaked eyelashes and bangs, Emma discerned a Washington State license plate. The passenger door flew open. She could hear *Take Me Home, Country Roads* playing on the radio in the cab. A big-boned woman in overalls and a baseball cap climbed down. Her boots touched down with a splash. The rig's turn signals flashed.

Slowly, the trucker approached the hyperventilating teenager. She held out a gentle, motherly hand of support.

"Oh, sweetie," the trucker said, "you're in a world of

hurt. Let me and my man take you to a hospital."

Emma collapsed into the woman's arms.

Despite her arthritic knees, the lady trucker ran up to the injured teen and caught her.

ONE

Deputy Glen Hart heard a scream carry loudly through the abandoned lot at Southeast Twenty-Eighth and Steele. It sounded more awkward and clumsy than terrified. Celebratory. Nevertheless, he set the textbook he'd been studying down on the white livery of his Dodge Charger's dashboard.

He was looking forward to delving into the next chapter, *Interrogation Techniques*. Simple concept, really.

Glen already possessed a sharp perception for reading a person's body language to discover their tell. Playing poker every weekend with his fellow police officers aided him in developing that skill.

He wiped the condensation off the windshield and scanned the area for any signs of trouble.

A couple of women in their twenties, a blonde and a brunette, were walking south with a drunken gait. Glen took them for a pair of college students heading back to their dorm after letting loose from their studies on a Friday night. The blonde filled out a crimson red sweatshirt snugly. Stitched letters made even bigger by her voluptuous figure spelled: R-E-E-D.

Glen allowed himself a smug grin at his deduction skills. He picked up his large coffee from the carrier in the center console below the onboard computer. After taking a big drink of the black, strong brew, Glen put the steaming cup back, then reached for the textbook. He peered at the clock radio; thirty minutes of his lunch break remained. Plenty of time to read a few more pages and scribble highlights down in his notebook.

His high school sweetheart and wife, Jenny, would tease him for not using the PalmPilot she'd given him on their ten-year anniversary.

He smiled at the college girls. As they got closer to the intersection they were howling and squealing. Glen remembered having good times like that in college. For a fleeting moment he thought about an old friend in his fraternity that he had a falling out with. The girls screamed some more, louder now. The blonde wrapped her arms around the redhead as if the ground had vanished beneath her feet. Glen hoped they didn't make enough racket to trip the sensitive motion sensors in the chiropractor clinic across the street.

The night shift's patrol duty was relaxing, overall, and he wanted it to stay that way.

He was watching the college girls jaywalk across the intersection towards 7-Eleven. He didn't need a radar gun to know that the muddy yellow pickup hauling ass down Steele was speeding. His cracked open passenger window vibrated from the subwoofers in their truck bellowing out a metal tune, while a whoosh of westerly wind ruffled his jet black hair. Glen spotted a gun rack with hunting rifles mounted. The truck came to a hard stop, brakes whining.

The passenger shoved his head out through the window. A swastika covered the back of his bald cranium.

Glen frowned in anger. He could think of nothing better than cracking that skull open like a hard-boiled egg.

"You stupid cunts," the Aryan yelled, "why don'tcha' watch where the fuck you're goin'?"

"Fuck you, ya' Nazi piece a' shit," the redhead yelled right back, throwing her middle finger up high. The girls were less than a foot away from stepping up onto the opposite curb.

The pickup driver revved the engine, drowning out the women's threatening voices.

Glen despised men that abused women or children. He flipped switches. The cherries on top of the patrol car rolled and screeched. The entire block lit up with a blue and red aura of *don't fuck with the law.*

The guy with the tattoo on his head jerked his face around to sneer at Glen. The cop glared right back. The Aryan's eyes widened. His muscular arm, every inch of flesh covered in tattoos, waved around to give Glen the finger. Then the bald-headed thug latched onto the doorframe because the driver tore away from the intersection in a sharp left turn. Heavy-duty radials screamed and smoked.

Glen scrunched his eyes at the Oregon license plate. He could only make out partial letters before the vehicle sped away.

The motion alarm in the clinic annunciated, shrieking throughout the slumbering neighborhood. In his rear view mirror, Glen saw lights in the apartment complex wink on.

Shit, so much for a peaceful night.

The garbled voice of a dispatcher came on, asking for what sounded like his handle. He turned up the radio, then unclipped the handset. Holding down the transmit button, he radioed dispatch and asked them to repeat the transmission.

"Officer Hart, we're patching in a call for you," the dispatcher said.

"Okay. Go."

"Officer Hart, this is Nurse Carpenter at North Providence. You're an emergency contact for Emma Rooney."

"Yes," he said. "She's my cousin. Is Emma—"

"Emma's in the ICU. She's been assaulted and raped."

"Oh God, no."

He dropped the handset and turned the Charger over. As he barreled north up Twenty-Eighth, Glen didn't bother to slow down for the speed bumps on the suburban streets. The metal undercarriage ground along the blacktop like Glen's teeth in his set jaw. He sped on behind the Fred Meyer Corporate Office Headquarters along Twenty-Sixth. More of the lights in their new five-story building were lit up.

A cop that wants to get somewhere fast doesn't travel in straight lines. Glen swerved around a Volvo stopped for the light at Powell, then made a wide left into thin late-night traffic. Burgerville's billboard boasted fresh peach milkshakes. He jagged right to pass a Ford puttering five miles under the speed limit in the fast lane.

Emma was hurt bad. He needed to be at her side and find out what the fuck happened.

●

Institutional white blurred in Glen's peripheral vision. He'd rushed past the packed admitting area in the emergency room and was sprinting down the hallway. As a police officer, Glen knew exactly which wing he needed to get to. He'd taken statements from hospital staff, rape victims, or witnesses there several times. On occasion he'd even run an errand to pick up evidence for forensics.

Anything he could do to make detective before thirty.

"Move!" Glen said as he barged through a morose group of visitors that looked like they were lost or didn't care to be there.

The corridors had never seemed so claustrophobic or long before.

A charge of adrenaline boosted his pace as he stormed across the sky bridge. Heavy rain pelted the window panes. Glen's ribs and side began to ache. He reminded himself to breathe.

Glen sidestepped out of the path of a wide-eyed janitor pushing a cleaning cart. He collided with a patient trying to walk on crutches. The elderly man smacked the linoleum.

He looked up at Glen with enraged, wrinkly eyes. "You asshole. I'll sue."

"Shit, I'm so sorry," he said, skidding to a stop. He bent over to help the patient up.

"What did you call me?" the cranky senior scolded. "Don't touch me."

Glen held his hands up in surrender before he whipped back around to start running again.

"Hey!" an orderly said as he swooped in to assist. "Take it easy. Mr. Curry, you know you're not supposed to be walking around without an escort."

Glen scurried away and burst onto the ward.

A candy-striper at the nurse's station stood up from her computer monitor. "Can I help you, officer?"

"My cousin, Emma," he said, pausing to catch his breath, "Rooney—"

Glen bowed his head so he wouldn't cough into the woman's heart-shaped face. He'd given up smoking after college; smoked his last pack at his bachelor party. The damage to his lungs had been done though, and the side effects always came back after a sprint.

She got him a paper cup of water from the cooler near row of filing cabinets. "Here, drink this and I'll look up her room number."

"Thanks," Glen said. He picked up the cup. His hands were shaky from adrenaline and a plethora of emotions flooding his body and soul. Water dribbled on the countertop.

Her delicate fingers click-clacked on the keyboard. Glen noticed that she wasn't using her fingertips, but the ends of her long manicured nails that were just as efficient.

"You two must be close," she said warmly.

"Yeah, I gave her her first stick driving lesson on our grandparents' farm."

"Hay season, right," the candy-striper commented. She struck the enter key, then studied the screen.

Glen nodded and sipped water. He heard a *ding* sound and spotted the large elevator slide open. A pair of women in scrubs wheeled a gurney out.

"She just left X-ray," the candy-striper informed Glen, only he'd rushed away from the station.

He recognized Emma's brunette locks spilled over the edge of the gurney. He fell in alongside, careful not to nudge it. One of the orderlies warned him to watch out anyway.

"I'm family," Glen said curtly.

Emma turned her head around at the sound of his voice.

Glen winced. Emma's face had been pulverized. Her right eye was swollen shut, the tissue of her eyelid the diameter of a golf ball. A metal splint covered her nose. Oxygen tubes ran from her nostrils. Knuckle marks had scuffed her wide cheekbones to bruise her fair skin black and blue. Dried blood caked her lips. A gash serrated her left earlobe from where an earring had been ripped out.

Tears oozed from Emma's left eye, an anguished pattern that made for a stark contrast over smeared makeup and scraped flesh.

"I'm here for you, Cuz," Glen said.

He reached for Emma's hand to squeeze it, but she curled it into a tight fist.

"I . . . I . . ." she wheezed. Her face scrunched with intense pain. She'd overheard the X-ray technician mention that several of her ribs were cracked. "I don't want you to see me like this."

"Emma . . . ?"

She turned her head. "Go away," Emma wept. "Leave me alone."

Glen skidded to a halt as the scrubs wheeled her into a recovery room. The woman pushing the foot of the gurney stopped to kick the door stop up and shut the door.

She made eye contact before the gap closed. "She'll be alright. We'll take good care of her."

Glen watched them move the gurney alongside the bed. As one of the scrubs lowered the railing to begin the transfer, the other one wheeled a privacy screen around to obfuscate the view into shadows.

Shoulders slumped, Glen reflected how his training as a cop didn't prepare him to stand in the shoes of a victim, or a loved one helpless to prevent the crime. He felt sharp nails touch his bicep through his sweat-soaked uniform. Glen spun around.

It gave the candy-striper a start. The clipboard in her hand fell.

Glen bent his knees and stooped down. He clutched the clipboard before it could smack the linoleum. He apologized and stood back up, slowly. For a second he admired her beautiful legs. He offered the board back.

"It's for you, actually," she said. "Would you mind filling out the paperwork?"

"Sure. Can you please get a message to Emma's doctor that I'd like to speak with him?"

"Of course, Officer Hart."

"Just call me Glen."

"Tiffany," she said.

"Thanks, Tiffany."

She returned to the nurse's station.

Glen headed for the waiting area. He ducked into the bathroom. Disinfectant stung his nose and tear ducts that ached to purge, but this wasn't the time. Setting the clipboard on top of the paper towel dispenser, he washed his face off.

His cell phone rang and he answered it.

"Why the hell did you abandon your patrol, Hart?" Sergeant Lou Mulgrew asked.

Glen explained the family emergency.

"Do what you have to do, son. Next time, though, use the radio."

"Yes, sir."

"Call me if you need anything, Hart."

Glen cleared his throat. "I'm going to need a couple days."

"I don't like the sound of that, son."

"It's just to watch over Emma," Glen lied.

His imagination was ablaze with violent images of what he wanted to do to the bastards that'd sexually assaulted his little cousin.

"Time off isn't the problem," Mulgrew said. "It's that sullen pitch of vengeance I hear in your voice. We'll talk soon."

The sergeant ended the call.

Glen shoved the phone back into his pocket. He mumbled curse words and scowled at his reflection in the mirror.

Fuck that, he thought, *I'm not going to just stand by and do nothing.*

Emma deserved justice.

Glen meandered over to the waiting room. On his way there he passed a vending nook. A fat woman in overalls was perusing the junk food. The space wasn't big enough for Glen to get in and grab a quick soda. She grabbed a soiled dollar bill from her pocket. Once her stubby fingers straightened out the currency she fed it into the machine. The bill rolled back out like an obstinate child sticking out its tongue.

Glen couldn't wait. He moved into the waiting room. He unsheathed his nightstick and plopped down in a padded wooden chair. He set the club down amidst the back issues of *Newsweek* and *National Geographic* strewn on the coffee table in front of him. He rapidly scribbled information down on Emma's paperwork in block letters. Just on the other side of the table, a big guy in baggy blue jeans and an even baggier Hawaiian shirt was laid out on the couch, snoring. Every now and then a hair of his immaculately-trimmed chevron mustache tickled his nose and hushed his snoring, but not enough to wake him up. He reeked of nicotine and made Glen think about lighting up a smoke.

Glen scrawled his signature on the last line. He tried calling Emma's parents and voicemail answered. He'd already left two messages and chose not to leave a third. Where the hell could they be?

Standing up, Glen waited for the blood to flow through his legs, then slid the nightstick back into his belt. He wondered what bashing in the skulls of Emma's attackers could feel like.

He dropped the paperwork off at the nurse's station, and asked Tiffany if she'd heard anything from the doctor.

"I'm afraid not, Glen. He's going to be in the ER for hours. Three-car collision on Thirty-Ninth, near the highway exit."

The cop nodded sternly, then left.

TWO

In an alternate timeline where Emma wouldn't have been raped and the night's homecoming festivities had transpired as normal, arrangements had been made for her to sleep over at Glen and Jenny's place. In the morning Jenny would've made Emma's favorite breakfast: whole-wheat banana pancakes smothered with apple butter. The Harts would've been eager and supportive, listening to Emma go on-and-on about the party, the successes of her cheerleading squad, and her ex-boyfriend.

They'd just broken up, but for appearance's sake, and to maintain their friendship, Jake had agreed to escort Emma to homecoming. Emma wouldn't have been able to find another date at the last minute, and the captain of the squad showing up without one would've been an act of social suicide. Jake was supposed to drop her off at the Hart's home after a tailgate party.

So that's how Glen knew Jake's mobile number. He was calling it just a few minutes past the witching hour.

The jock's cocky message greeting came on. "You know what to do after the *beeeep*."

"You've got some explaining to do, Jake. Call me back before I have to come looking for your dumb ass,"

Glen said, leaving his fourth message in less than thirty minutes.

"Shit." He tossed his cell phone aside. It bounced off the passenger's seat and smacked the floorboard.

Smothered by anger and guilt, Glen almost sped right past his own house in Sellwood. He made a last-second course correction, and in a hairpin turn, pulled into the two-car driveway. Jenny always parked her BMW in the garage. The crime was frequent in their neighborhood. Crackheads broke the antenna off the jeep to utilize it as a single-use crack pipe. The vehicle jerked upward and something crunched under the right front wheel.

Christ, please don't let that be the stray cat Jenny feeds scraps to.

The impact didn't seem squishy enough to have been an animal. Then again, the way the night was going . . .

After retrieving his phone and clutching his gym bag, Glen hopped down from the jeep. On his way to the front door he paused and peered at the driveway entrance to see what he'd run over. Pumpkin chunks were strewn everywhere. Jenny was going to be pissed. The trio of jack o' lanterns she'd carved last weekend were crushed to pieces. At least he hadn't knocked over her hand-painted sign that bid trick r' treaters welcome in gruesome, cobwebbed Gothic lettering.

And it wasn't the damn cat either.

Glen heard Drake's loud bark through the door before his key slid into the deadbolt. Jenny ordered him to hush. Glen opened the door and hustled inside.

The aroma of garlic permeated the air. A television screen flickered in the dim light of the living room where a woman screamed in stereo. Glen's shoulders flinched.

"Aww . . ." his wife said affectionately, "did the scary movie frighten you?"

Jenny put a small glass dish of roasted pumpkin seeds down on the small end table by the recliner, then untucked her shapely legs out from underneath her lithe torso. The flames crackling in the fireplace between her and the idiot box lit up her wide cheekbones. Her nipples poked out beneath one of Glen's silky, black button-down dress shirts. Tiny black cats freckled her orange panties. Shifting her creamy green eyes away from the commercial break, Jenny stretched her body out in a seductive offering. The golden hue of the fire lightened her strands of waist-length, chestnut-colored hair into luxurious ribbons of smooth caramel elegance.

"Trick r' . . . Glen, what's wrong?"

He dropped his bag. Kicking the door shut with his heel, Glen rushed down the hallway off the kitchen and dining room.

Jenny bolted up from her chair and jogged after him. "What's wrong?"

"Emma's been raped, Jenny."

Her eyes widened and she covered the gasp rushing from her parted lips with her hand.

Glen went into the bedroom. While Jenny sat on their

king-sized bed, she watched her husband take off his uniform and dress down into black jeans, T-shirt, and boots.

"What are you going to do?" she said.

He clasped his belt and left the room. Jenny saw the light turn on in his den next door. She stood up and took baby steps out into the hallway.

She saw that the gun cabinet doors were opened. Glen clenched his Mossberg 500 pump action shotgun as he thumbed shells into the magazine tube. His eyes refused to meet her worried gaze. She heard the click of his finger switching the safety off.

"Glen, what the *fuck* are you going to do?!" she screamed.

He marched out of the den and ducked into Jenny's art room at the end of the hallway. Every inch of wall space was adorned with her framed pencil and ink illustrations that ranged from pretty flowers and provocative human subjects to majestic landscapes. It doubled as a guest room, complete with a twin bed and an antique bureau that Glen had restored. He opened the top drawer. It contained assorted articles of Emma's clothing left behind from previous sleepovers. He grabbed a pair of panties and stuffed them into his pocket.

"Drake and I are going hunting," Glen said bluntly.

"Where are you going to start?" Jenny asked.

"With that quarterback asshole, Jake. I'll make him take me to where the tailgate party was held. Drake will pick up Emma's scent from there."

Jenny followed Glen back to the living room. "Then what?"

"Find the bastards that raped my little cousin and maybe ram this 12 gauge up their asses."

The television station announced, *"Now, back to Wes Craven's The Last House on the Left."*

Glen whistled. "Come here, Drake! Come here, boy!"

The bloodhound mastiff's head reared up fast. Drake shot from his bed near Jenny's chair. He circled around Glen and immediately began to sniff at the air. Glen petted Drake's fawn coat enthusiastically. Drake barked with purpose and drooled all over Glenn's boots.

"That's a *good* dog. Yes . . ."

"This is a bad idea," Jenny said.

"What the hell else am I supposed to do? Wait to hear about the suspects being caught on the news? She's my cousin, dammit."

"For Chrissake, ease up, Glen," she said. "You're a police officer."

"Not tonight." He picked up his gym bag. "I'll check in before dinner."

Glen kissed his wife goodbye and opened the door to leave. They stepped out onto the stoop. A floodlight in front of the house clicked on and shined directly in their astonished faces. Drake barked rapidly.

Racking the slide, Glen aimed the Mossberg just a few inches above the powerful light. His index finger moved from outside the trigger guard to curl around the trigger. Jenny dropped to her knees and covered both ears. Welcome mat bristles chafed her skin.

"Who goes there?" Glen shouted.

White spots were floating on the edge of his vision. He could make out the outline of a pickup truck and a large man. Puffs of cold breath or smoke drifted up into the atmosphere and dissipated. Glen took a deep breath to steady the waves of adrenaline flooding his body.

He inhaled a nauseous cigar odor he'd last smelled at a department BBQ last summer.

"Lou, is that you?" he asked the massive silhouette.

"I cut my fishing trip short. Put that scatter gun down before you do something we both regret, Hart," Sergeant Mulgrew said in his Western drawl.

Glen lowered the weapon.

Mulgrew stepped out from behind the light. He had on waders and a flannel shirt. Pushing paper had chained him to a desk and pronounced his beer belly, but his large hands were the paws of a black bear.

"Stand up, Jenny," Mulgrew said. "Why don't you go inside so your husband and I can sort this matter out."

The masculine sound of Mulgrew's resonant voice reminded Jenny of Sam Elliott. She stood up and huddled close to Glen.

He shook his head. "You can hear this, too. I don't keep secrets from my wife, Lou."

"Fair enough. What the hell are you up to, Hart?

Shouldn't you be at the hospital, watching over your cousin?"

"Thought I'd do a little deer hunting," Glen said.

"With a shotgun," Mulgrew chuckled, then the laughter dropped off abruptly. "Bullshit."

An uncomfortable silence of despair lingered in the drizzling rain.

Mulgrew broke it and said, "Remember your oath."

"To uphold the law," Hart said. "Where does that leave Emma though? She's wired up to a bed. Beaten. Broken. Soaked in blood and semen."

Slowly, the senior police officer walked forward, closing the distance between himself and the finest deputy he'd ever trained. He could see the kid making captain someday.

"The sex offenders that did it will be caught," Mulgrew assured, "and the justice system will seal their fate. Not a rogue cop forsaking his code for vigilantism. You've got one helluva career path in front of you. Don't stray off it for revenge."

Mulgrew placed his hand on the Mossberg, clicked the safety on.

Glen slumped forward. He sniffled up tears in the cold dampness. His lower lip quivered. Droplets of moisture beaded his moody eyebrows.

"Let it go, son." The sergeant took the gun out of Glen's loosened grip, then patted him on the shoulder. "Good man. I'm going to hold onto this for a few days.

Jenny, get him inside. Keep each other warm tonight."

As she fastened the deadbolt, Jenny heard the engine in Mulgrew's rig turn over. She bent forward to turn the television off.

"Hold it," Glen said. "Is this about the criminals that rape and murder two girls, then stay in a house nearby to get out of a storm? Only the occupants are the parents of one of the girls, and they avenge their daughter."

"Yeah, I think so."

They snuggled up on the love seat next to the recliner and finished watching the movie. Drake fell asleep curled up in his bed. He snored so loud that Jenny had to turn up the volume. As the credits began to roll, the beeps of Glen's cell phone ringing perforated their all-too-brief alone time. He released a long exhale before answering it.

Now what?

Seconds after the call ended, Glen dropped the handset. The calm in his face gave way to a look of anguish as his eyes shut. He couldn't restrain his sorrow any longer and wept. Jenny hugged and soothed him to find out what happened. Emma's folks had been struck by a three-car collision on their way to the hospital.

They were dead on arrival.

THREE

November, 2010

The pythons hissing and slithering in their aquarium didn't wake up Izabella Sommer. Neither did her chinchilla, Mia. The industrial, post-grunge metal that blasted through Izabella's earbuds telling her it was 4 A.M. and time to get ready for work, did. The curious, spunky rodent played with the red satin curtains, parting them enough for a ray from a streetlight in the back alley to concentrate directly over the pulled out futon.

Izabella reached behind her head for the cell phone on the nightstand to shut the alarm off. She tugged the buds out and tossed them aside. Her girlfriend, Amanda, stirred. Izabella snuggled up against Amanda's warm, supple skin. She adored the freckles that dotted Amanda's shoulder blades like a constellation.

"Don't get up. Sleep in. Make yourself at home," she muttered in Amanda's ear, then kissed her cheek. "Dream about me."

Amanda mumbled okay.

Rolling out of bed, Izabella crept into the foyer. She entered the bathroom. Izabella flipped on the light. A cockroach the size of a long manicured fingernail skittered around the sink basin and escaped down the drain.

She freshened up with a quick shower. Her brown, waist-length dreadlocks would go another day without being submerged, so she merely dampened them a bit, and squirted a few drops of tea tree oil into the roots. While moving around in the needle spray she bumped the wire mesh basket full of lemons that hung from a hook. Izabella grabbed a cake of rosemary-scented soap and lathered up. The last flakes of dead skin from the latest tattoo on her left hand, a red rose in full bloom, washed away. After rinsing the suds off her athletic body, she stepped out of the tub.

Gently, she patted her mastectomy scars dry, followed by her heart-shaped face. An array of piercings emphasized Izabella's Danish-Swedish features: Sterling silver curved barbells off-center in her eyebrows, a titanium D-ring hung on the bridge of her nose, an ouroboros through her septum, and two loops hugging her lower lip near the corners of her mouth.

The surgical steel twinkled in the incandescent lighting. A beauty mark on her left cheek offset the modifications.

Returning to the bedroom, Izabella rifled through the chest of drawers and closet. She put on a pair of thermal socks, Hanes charcoal boxer briefs, and a gray tank top. She wrapped up her wardrobe with black, patched-up jeans and a too-tight, red and black-checkered flannel shirt. One of the patches on the seat of the pants read *I ♥ LESBIANS*. Another repair on the right back pocket featured a swastika with a strike through it and a statement that quantified the message. *NAZI PUNKS FUCK OFF*.

By now, the aroma of drip coffee that'd brewed on a timer permeated the one-bedroom apartment. Izabella moved over to the kitchenette off the main room. The fish tank in the entertainment center where most people would keep a TV provided adequate illumination for Izabella to go about her morning routine. She dumped a cup of old-fashioned oats in a chipped blue mug, covered the oats with water, and nuked them for a couple minutes. Izabella took her coffee black. Once the microwave beeped, she removed the steaming mug, and topped the oats with a handful of blueberries and a dollop of almond milk. Izabella sat at the small round table between the counter and refrigerator and ate her breakfast.

The oats were a little overcooked, chewy. Sips of the hot Guatemalan java washed them down easily. In between spoonfuls Izabella scrolled through her smartphone. She perused some local news, and checked her calendar for Saturday's appointments and events.

GRIZZLY DISCOVERY OF BLACK MARKET SURGICAL THEATER

Izabella had a strong stomach, but she kept flipping to the next article. She couldn't read about that shit while she was eating.

BLOOD BANK BREAK IN

She scraped the container to spoon up every last hearty, nutritious morsel. A blueberry seed wedged between her teeth. Izabella set the mug in the sink to soak. After returning to the bathroom, she brushed and flossed.

Hiking boots pulled on and laced up tight, Izabella grabbed her house keys and chained wallet out of a white ceramic bowl. It occupied a shelf with a pair of leafy bamboo stocks in a square glass planter full of pebbles, and a framed photograph of her and Amanda. She stuffed the key and hemp billfold in her left side pocket, then clipped the chain to a belt loop.

The photograph immortalized the happy couple posing semi-naked in front of a snowman. They'd built it last winter while staying at a timeshare cabin in the northern wilderness of Norway. For the eyes they had used the spare buttons from their matching flannel shirts, while their favorite gel dildo provided the jolly figure with a ridiculous schnoz. White briefs on Izabella and panties with tiny candy canes on Amanda showed off their legs. Izabella remembered the warmth in her belly after slugging back true shots of cinnamon whiskey.

Izabella touched her lips and pressed her fingers to Amanda's face on the picture. She left and locked up.

The youth sports center across the street from the brownstone she called home was still cordoned off with crime scene tape. She'd been out the night the violence occurred, but Izabella heard stories from patrons in the late-night speakeasy that occupied the basement of her building.

Izabella didn't care much for sensational gossip, but the bar served up the most crispy and delicious beer-battered onion rings in town. All she knew for certain was that the trouble had decimated a neighborhood gym. It also happened in close proximity to her place. If it was time to move out, relocating could put a strain on her relationship.

Two blocks northwest, Izabella traipsed into the parking lot at the southeast corner of Grand and Belmont. Six cars were in line for the Green Beans coffee cart.

She heard Emma Rooney's contagious laughter and smiled. They'd met at a grief counseling group so it was always a treat to know there could be more to her than depression. Emma was an all-around good person, a terrific barista, and a helluva sketch artist.

She'd drawn the floral stencil inked on Izabella's hand.

However, Izabella felt a darkness emanating from Emma's soul. The inner turmoil reminded Izabella of the breast cancer that took her mom's life too soon. Although both of them had recently lost close relatives to cancer, Izabella elected for breast removal, then entered into a relationship to rebuild her life, while Emma continued to visit her stepmother's gravesite every Monday afternoon for lengthy conversations.

Healthy, sure. Everyone did that. But it seemed to Izabella that Emma needed to move on.

Their friendship was branching off onto different paths.

Izabella climbed into the company panel truck that contained all the tools and supplies for her part-time job when she wasn't modeling or tattooing. She unlocked her phone, tapped up the mail from her supervisor with the work order attached. The address indicated she needed to head for the entrance to the Brooklyn Yard where Southeast Twenty-Second Avenue became Gladstone. Izabella started the engine and rolled out onto Taylor Street.

Shirley Manson rocked the alternative airwaves, singing *I'm Only Happy When It Rains* as a torrential downpour began to fall. Izabella smirked, tapping the steering wheel to the beat.

"This should be Portland's theme song."

She turned right onto Twenty-Second. The red leaves still clinging to the trees that bordered Cleveland Park were transforming into a rusty orange. Izabella spotted teenagers raking up dead leaves into piles. An elderly transient in a plastic poncho, hunched over, pushed his cart of belongings along the sidewalk. The buggy doubled as a walker. Everything he owned was getting soaked.

Except for a few cars parked near the main five-story building, the Fred Meyer Corporate Headquarters parking lot was nearly deserted. An overweight security guard tooled around in a green golf cart, making rounds of the premises.

A few more yards up the street and on her right, she glanced at the retaining wall that lead toward the Brooklyn Yard entrance. Graffiti covered the cracked concrete surface. The obscure signature she'd spray painted there in her teens had long since been painted over by someone else's impression.

Izabella flinched as she heard a loud horn blare and rubber screech pavement. Out of the corner of her eye she saw the semi truck, hauling freight, rolling down Gladstone. They were on a collision course for the same destination. Izabella floored the brake. The panel truck shimmied to an abrupt stop.

She looked up at the truck driver. He was making enraged gestures at her with pudgy sausages. Izabella allowed the road rage to slide and waved for the asshole to go first. He moved on, flipping Izabella off as he passed by.

Giving the trucker a shit-eating grin, she said, "Gee, so many gentlemen in this backwater town."

Izabella's Scandinavian accent flared up.

She pulled over for other vehicles to drive around her. This side street detour sure routed a lot more traffic lately. Especially big rigs. Izabella switched her flashers on and waited for the truck to advance. She listened to three grunge hits from the nineties. The deejay referring to them as 'oldies' pissed off a listener that called into the radio station to rant.

Izabella grinned in amusement. Grunge *was* old. So were hippies from the sixties and the punks from the seventies. All were identifiable and sustainable lifestyles, though. And they were all alive and thriving in Portland. In order to prove it, Izabella merely had to look in a mirror or pose for a camera.

The semi truck's Mack engine roared as it cleared the gate. Izabella drove up. A lean, tall security guard hustled out of the shack close by, a clipboard of papers tucked underneath his armpit. Rain drenched his baseball cap and beads of water dripped from the brim. He jogged around to the driver's side of the panel truck. Izabella rolled the window down. Cigarettes and strong coffee tainted his breath.

"How can I help you?" he said.

Izabella flashed her smartphone screen with the work order displayed to the guard. "The name's Izabella Sommer. I'm with Aftermath Cleaners."

The guard didn't bother with double-checking his printouts. "Oh yeah . . . You're here for the blue cargo container. You're a little early."

"I just want to get this dirty work done so I can enjoy the rest of the day," she said.

He pointed north and told Izabella to look for the crime scene tape wrapped around the doors. She thanked the guard and entered the train yard. The atmosphere was thick with odors of gasoline, oil, and damp steel. Izabella switched the radio off. She kept her eyes peeled for the blue container, while she navigated through the industrial terrain, and watched out for forklifts, trains, or trucks.

She parked next to the blue container. Hopping out, Izabella moved to the back of the panel truck. She unlatched and shoved the roll up door open. She braced her knee on the lift platform and scrambled inside. She closed the door to change. A few minutes later the door rolled back up.

Izabella jumped down in disposable booties. She wore a white hazmat suit. Black rubber gloves were strapped on over the sleeves of the suit. To complete the protective outfit, she fastened an air purifying mask over her mouth and nose, then lowered a shield over her face.

Izabella nonchalantly tossed a large trash bag over her shoulder. She untangled the crime scene tape from the doors. Putting some elbow grease into her grip, she unlatched them and pulled one open.

Her vision adjusted to the darkness. The stench hit her. Izabella rapidly backed up a few steps, flipped the face shield up, then ripped the air mask off. Gagging, she bent over and vomited. The sour glob of half-absorbed blueberries and oats splattered the concrete.

Izabella wiped her mouth. Once she steadied herself, she walked back up to the cargo container entrance and looked inside. Her brown eyes widened, taking in the macabre site.

Blood smeared every square foot and spattered the walls. Voids in the sticky mess revealed where the legs of an operating table used to sit. Forensics left an evidence marker behind.

Izabella didn't need to bother reading about the discovery of the black market surgical theater. She had to clean it up.

FOUR

"Using beeswax to make dreads is a bad idea," Naomie said as she steamed some milk. "It doesn't wash out."

Emma and Naomie had spotted Izabella getting into her company vehicle earlier during their shift.

The bronze-skinned, part-time barista and hairdresser had just returned from a vacation in Greece. She loved all of the historical artifacts in the museums there that proved dreadlocks were a popular hairstyle centuries ago.

Naomie's trip represented somewhat of a pilgrimage to her place of origin. Her Jamaican and Scottish parents got pregnant with her there while on their honeymoon.

"By the way," she said, "everyone at the salon asked me to give you a hug for participating at the Locks for Cancer fundraiser last month."

"I was happy to contribute," Emma said, then put on a boo-boo lip. "I just hope it grows back before winter sets in."

Emma appreciated the small talk with her co-workers at the coffee cart. It provided her with positive vibes to focus on when negativity threatened her cool persona. Not that she didn't possess a valid reason to snap.

For instance, at the many men that leered at her while asking for her phone number, or the guys that undressed her with lingering gazes. Currently, an asshole actually had the sick nerve to waggle his tongue at her as if he knew the proper way to give a woman oral pleasure.

Emma fought the urge to jump through the drive-thru window, and stab his tongue with her pencil. In between orders, Emma doodled and sketched random objects in a 5X7 leather bound book. Filling the blank pages kept her mental agility fluid and sharp.

Carefully, she handed the sexist pig his large, extra-hot, quad shot, low-fat caramel macchiato. "Thank you," she said with a nice smile. "Have an awesome day."

Emma handled the drink by holding the cup. The scumbag tried gripping the lid where it sealed between his fingers. Little did he know that Emma selected a lid that'd rested on top of a heat source for too long.

He pulled forward, and tilted the cup to take a drink. The melted lid popped right off. Hot coffee splashing in his lap, the sex fiend screamed from his crotch burning.

Emma relished the moment. Until his car braked. Maybe he intended to back up and complain, but there were four cars waiting behind him, and Naomie had her hands full with three customers that just moseyed over to the walk up window.

The motorist in the gray Dodge Charger behind the tongue-wagger's car honked his horn.

"Move it," he yelled. "Some of us are on lunch break

and have a job to get back to."

Oh shit, Emma thought. *I know that voice.*

The Charger pulled up to Emma's window.

"Hey, Cuz," Glen said. "You don't return my voicemails or texts, so here I am."

Emma would have actually preferred to deal with the sexist pig than with her cousin and former guardian.

"Hi," she said politely. "Welcome to Green Beans. What can I brew for you today?"

"Come on . . . Don't be like that."

"Would you like to try one of the specials?" Emma said, pointing at the chalkboard mounted beside the window.

"No, I need your help for something else," Glen said. "It's a case, Emma."

"I'm sorry, *Sir*, but if you're not going to buy a tasty beverage, I need to ask you to leave. There are paying customers waiting behind you."

"Emma . . . *Please.*"

She grinned. "This reminds me of the time when I begged you to help me convince the county not to fire all the forensic sketch artists due to budget cuts, and you let me down."

Naomie's attention and curiosity perked up faster than a college student pounding energy drinks to pull an all-nighter. "Whaaat?" she asked, her untamable shock of black curly hair bouncing.

"Jesus H. Christ," he said. "You know I was grieving

at the time."

"We both were, Glen." One of the customers in line leaned on their horn. "Make your choice."

A stiff wind blew through the strands of Emma's long, straightened candy apple red hair and whirled it about like fire ignited on a torch.

"Fine. Just give me a large drip coffee. Cream and sugar."

●

Later on, after business slowed down a little, Naomie fired off a volley of questions. "Who was that guy that said he's your cousin? Were you really a forensic whatchamacallit? Did you ever help catch a criminal?"

Emma thought her friend needed to switch to decaf.

"Glen's a captain in the tri-county major crimes division of the Portland Police Bureau."

"I should've known," Naomie said. "He sounds like an asshole."

Emma's relief arrived and it was the end of her shift.

"I'll tell you about the rest some other time," she said, grabbing her bag to rush off to job number two. She jockeyed a cash register at Trader Joe's. "Maybe at the gym tomorrow."

Naomie gave her a hug. "Okay. See ya'. 7 A.M. sharp. Last one there—"

"Buys breakfast," Emma finished.

After the county had laid her off, Emma realized that she needed to work three jobs just to pay the rising rent.

Never mind the debts she was still paying off for legal and mortuary fees. She needed a break. Hell, a vacation would be nice. But not in this lifetime.

Her next shift didn't begin for two hours. Plenty of time to sit down, relax, reflect, and get a bite to eat. She went to Rice Junkies on Hawthorne. Carbs fueled her thoughts, while the calming Asian decor kept her bad memories in perspective.

●

Glen kicked the swinging double doors to the Major Crimes squad room open. Since it was a Saturday afternoon, the cubicles were virtually empty. Married detectives with kids or spouses took weekends off to spend time with family. On the way to his office, Glen walked around.

Heather MacGraw's desk remained vacated. A grin curved up the corner of his mouth. He got a kick out of all the decorative memorabilia from her days as a cheerleader at U of O. A statue of 'The Duck' sat next to her flatscreen monitor. The mascot made an O for Oregon with his hands. Heather showed off a lot of spirit.

She'd been on suspension since the stunt she pulled with Matt Grudge and Leslie Crow at the Brooklyn Yard. They'd discovered the surgical bay in the container, but it interfered with federal jurisdiction, and garnered unnecessary attention from the media. Union members argued how the destruction of property and the overuse of violence compromised shipping deadlines. Last night a bicycle courier delivered a registered envelope from an independent attorney to Glen. It contained the notice of a wrongful death suit against the department brought on by the parents of one of the gangbangers Heather shot in self defense at the yard. The mayor cried about the incident putting holiday tourism at risk.

Heather couldn't return to work until December 10th.

Glen sipped his coffee. The java warmed his bones. Now that he was entering his forties, Glen was beginning to experience aches in some of his joints. Hot beverages soothed the pain.

He stopped at Detective Walton's cubicle. The younger man was interviewing a bank manager. The bank he worked at was robbed two weeks ago, and a security guard had been shot in the face. A teller was permanently maimed. Unfortunately, the video surveillance had been down for maintenance. Walton was utilizing facial reconstruction software to generate an image of the suspect.

Walton clicked and scrolled through a multitude of features as he asked the witness, "How about this nose? Did it look like this? Maybe this one . . ."

The portly manager looked at his watch, then rubbed his eyes to stay awake. "The nose was flat, like it'd been broken a lot. Yeah, that one."

"You're sure?" Walton coaxed.

"Yes. Wait . . . Now the eyes are wrong."

Walton sighed and re-selected the eyes.

"How's it going?" Glen asked.

The detective nodded at his captain with encouragement, while the witness shrugged wearily.

"Mr. Perry," Glen said, "thank you for coming in on the weekend for an interview. Away from the usual hustle and bustle of this department, we're counting on your concentration and memory to identify the suspect."

"I'm happy to help," the round-faced bank manager said. He took his glasses off to clean them. "After shooting Burt, the son of a bitch splashed Sarina's face with a baby food jar full of acid. Oh, Jesus . . ." A tear coasted down his cheek and the witness lowered his head to hide his traumatic sorrow.

"Let's take a moment," Walton said. "Maybe get some coffee. Starbucks. My treat."

"Good idea," Glen said. "I'll be in my office all afternoon if you need anything."

"Thanks, Captain Hart," Walton said, escorting the witness away from the harsh enquiry.

As his detective and the bank manager walked out of the squad room, Glen overheard Walton engaging Perry with everyday chit-chat. It could help bring Perry's recollection of the killer's face to life.

"So, Mr. Perry, what do you do when you're not managing the bank? Do you like any sports?"

"Except for the Olympics, not so much," the bank manager said. "I collect classical music, opera mostly."

Walton's idea of great music was blasting Nickelback

while he worked out or hosted backyard barbecues at his home. "Oh . . . That sounds like an interesting hobby."

The detective's rapport with the witness plummeted.

Glen shook his head and walked into his office. He wanted to eat his lunch before it got any colder than this case.

The fluorescent lights brought out more of the white than black in Glen's salt-and-pepper crew cut. He removed his damp overcoat and hung it on the rack in the corner by the door. Glen pulled his beige corduroy suit jacket off to drape it over the back of the swivel chair behind his desk. It was his favorite jacket. Jenny had found it at the Salvation Army. The elbows had been reinforced with patches. But the best alteration Jenny made was tailoring the fit to conceal his sidearm, which he wore in a shoulder rig.

Sitting down, Glen loosened his tie and unfolded the brown bag. He shoved stacks of files aside to make room, then removed the contents to place them on the blotter. Two photographs in matted, hand-carved wooden frames reminded him of the duty and love he strived for as a police officer. One of Glen during a log drill at Marine Corps boot camp, and Jenny posing for a glamour portrait before chemo took her hair. Glen unwrapped his sandwich, a tuna melt on whole wheat, and took a bite. He closed his eyes, chewing on the moist fish and sharp cheddar. Spoon in hand, he pulled the cloudy lid off the bowl. Steam arose from the creamy chicken vegetable soup.

As he dug in and raised a bite to his mouth the telephone rang.

Glen put the spoon down and answered the call.

"Major Crimes. Captain Hart here."

The receptionist informed Glen he had a visitor. Maybe it was Emma. He jumped out of the chair and bumped the desk. Some of the soup spilled. Riding the elevator down, Glen stared at the digital floor number display, willing it to go faster.

When he reached the lobby, Glen skidded to a halt. His shoulders hunched down in disappointment.

Izabella Sommer was leaning against the front desk, decked out in full punk regalia. She wore the scrappy clothes, the feral hair, and the piercings proudly. Glen respected that. Aside from being comfortable in her skin and gay lifestyle though, Izabella was just another dumb ass that dropped out of college to pursue modeling instead.

"You were expecting someone else," she said.

Glen approached and offered her a handshake.

The crime scene cleaner ignored the courteous greeting, and handed over two plastic bags.

"What's this?"

Glen held the sealed bags up to the light. He could make out an evidence marker in one, but the other item required harder scrutiny.

"It's an empty blood bag left at the scene. I found

it on top of the container. I e-mailed you time-stamped pictures of the discovery to preserve the chain of evidence."

"I appreciate that, Izabella. Thanks."

"If there's nothing else," she said, "I'm outta' here."

"Wait a minute," Glen touched her shoulder. Izabella scowled at his hand and he dropped it. "Do you still moonlight as a nude life model at the art course Emma teaches? If you see her can you ask Emma to call me, please?"

"Yeah, I'll deliver the message, but I wouldn't be surprised if she told you to fuck off," Izabella informed the detective in a gruff tone.

"Thanks a bunch," Glen said, voice raised. He breathed the air between them. "Now get the hell outta' here. You stink."

"Happily," Izabella said, staring at the cop's back with hatred in her eyes as he walked away.

She sniffed at her shoulder. Dammit, the asshole was right.

She reeked of death.

Izabella returned to her apartment. Stepping into a shower, she halved lemons and squeezed the juice into her dreads.

FIVE

Emma scanned a regular customer's package of spaghetti, a jar of marinara, ground beef, and a bottle of Charles Shaw Merlot. The inexpensive wine was known as "Two Buck Chuck." Emma preferred the Chardonnay herself and thought of buying a bottle to take home.

"Looks like it's Italian night at your place," Emma said.

"Do you want to come over for dinner?" her next door neighbor, Angel, asked. "Don't take this the wrong way, but I think you could use a hearty meal to put some meat on your bones. Besides, Athena is visiting her dad, and I could use the company. Business at the music store has been kind of slow."

"Can I get a rain check?" Emma said. "I've got to go to bed early for kickboxing in the morning."

"Anytime, girlfriend. Goodnight."

Angel always paraded around town wearing her handmade accessories. Her brown and orange mittens were knitted out of yarn. When Jenny wasn't instructing Emma on how to illustrate faces, she taught her crochet. Angel picked up her groceries and left.

The rank pot odor emanating from the next customer

almost gave Emma a contact high. His basket was loaded with snacks. He likely wore sunglasses in the overcast weather because his pupils were dilated.

"Hey, beautiful," the stoner said. "I'm throwing a special party tonight. Wanna' come?"

Emma pretended to consider the invitation as she double-bagged the groceries. *Ooo, chocolate chip cookies with walnuts.* "No, thanks."

"Peace out," he said and strutted off.

The third person wore a hoodie. Emma scanned two bottles of Charles Shaw Chardonnay.

"Did you find everything you needed?"

"One of those bottles is for you," Glen said, then pulled the hood down from his head. "So is this."

He placed an envelope down on the counter.

Emma's jaw set. She bagged both bottles of wine. Maintaining her composure because she couldn't afford to lose her temper or her job, Emma bid Glen a goodnight through clenched teeth.

"You know how to contact me if you reconsider," Glen told her as he took the sack and left.

Emma managed to power through the grief during the remainder of her shift. She forfeited her break to concentrate entirely on work instead of her estranged past with Glen. Her memory flashed images of her and Jenny staying up late, drinking Charles Shaw Chardonnay (Jenny's favorite wine, too), while they sketched together. The assistant manager rang her up a bottle.

"Hey, you okay?" Christa asked.

"Yeah, I'm good." Emma lied.

She exited the store and heard Christa lock the doors behind her. Emma hustled across the lot through pouring rain. She fell into the seat of her car, which was parked near a line of trees. Rain pounded the roof. The naked branches swaying in the wind mimicked tortured ghosts. She remembered walking out of the woods the night she was raped and how helpless she'd felt. Slumping forward, Emma hit the dashboard with her fists and wept until the windows fogged up.

She reached down in the backseat floorboard behind her for a Kleenex. Emma dried her swollen eyes and winced at her reflection in the rear view mirror. Her mascara was running.

Emma snatched the envelope. She tore it open with her fingernails. The photo she pulled out made her gasp.

It showed an olive-skinned woman lying in a hospital burn unit. The victim's face was bandaged, but Emma could see her melted, ravaged flesh creeping out from beneath the cotton. She shuddered.

"*Jesus* . . . Who did this?"

Emma started to slide the picture in the envelope when she saw the notes jotted down on the back. Glen's dark, heavy penmanship read:

SARINA, 23, TELLER
BANK ROBBER THREW ACID IN HER FACE

VISION AND VOCAL CORDS DESTROYED

VIDEO SURVEILLANCE AT SCENE
COMPROMISED

FACIAL RECONSTRUCTION SOFTWARE FAIL

BANK MANAGER WILLING TO WORK WITH
<u>**A SKETCH ARTIST**</u>

Emma dug her cell phone out of her bag and called Glen. He answered on the first ring. She cut him off before he could so much as say hello or speak her name.

"Alright, I'll do it," she said, then hung up.

●

Circling industrial and residential blocks, Emma eventually found a spot on Twenty-Fourth and Cora to parallel park. She stepped out of her car and walked north through a light drizzle. A gray beanie kept her head dry. At Twenty-Fifth and Gladstone she entered the Grrrl Power Gym.

The second hand on the clock above the free weights clicked past 7 A.M. Julie Ryan, one of the owners and trainers, greeted Emma boisterously as she hefted a jug of water onto the cooler.

"Lil' Emmers, how the fuck are ya'?!"

The filthy language didn't phase the two women sparring with rubber knives.

Emma hated that nickname, but she knew Julie meant it affectionately. She waved and yawned a good morning in return. Emma hadn't gotten to sleep as early last night as she'd intended. Online research about the bank robbery had kept her up past midnight. Yanking the beanie off, she ducked into the locker room.

"Argh, you beat me here," she said. "I guess breakfast is on me."

"Damn right it is," Naomie said as she wrapped her hands with athletic tape and gauze.

She was sitting on the bench beneath her locker. A plum sports bra supported her firm, voluptuous breasts. Black mini board shorts with teeny white skulls showed off her muscular legs.

"Don't pull your punches," Emma said, spinning the combination dial on her locker across from Naomie's.

"Are you certain you want that hard of a workout?" Naomie said. "I know the last few days have been rough on you."

Emma stowed her frayed, black denim jacket, then started to take off the rest of her clothes. Underneath a pink Bikini Kill tank top she already had on a glossy red sports bra. She forcefully unfastened her low rise, acid-washed jeans and shoved the snug material below her hips, then down to her ankles. Emma stuffed them in her locker. She completed her kick boxer attire by pulling up a pair of floral lace short shorts.

"I need to fight through it," Emma told her.

Naomie nodded solemnly. She set her gloves down on the bench, then shut the locker door.

Emma was wrapping up her hands. "Shit."

"What's wrong?" Naomie whipped around.

The padding slipped off Emma's knuckles.

Naomie stood toe-to-toe with her BFF. She held Emma's hand in her palm. "Let a sister help you out."

Emma craned her head upward. Naomie towered at six foot, three. "Thanks."

"No problem," Naomie said, unraveling the gold elastic to start over. "Well, for starters, you've got to wrap it around your wrist tight so the impact of a punch is absorbed through your arm instead of tweaking your wrist. We want to take care of those hands if you intend to keep drawing with them." She wound the wrap around Emma's knuckles and thumb. "There, all done. Isn't that better?"

Emma paid close attention so she could wrap her other hand herself.

"What's eating at you, anyway?" Naomie asked.

The sketch artist's imagination flashed on the corrosive wounds that'd condemned Sarina Bassim to live the rest of her life looking like a monster.

"I'm going to help Glen profile a violent crime suspect," Emma said.

"I've always ben curious about how you got started in that line of work. I didn't want to pry though, because I thought it involved Jenny."

"After the rape and my parents died, Glen and Jenny raised me. She trained me to be her successor."

"Well, I think she'd be very proud of you," Naomie said. "You're turning your focus outward and helping someone out. Give that victim mentality a kick in the ass."

Emma smirked, putting her gloves on. "Just as soon as I kick yours first."

"Now we're talking," Naomie cheered. "Bring it on."

They touched gloves, then walked out onto the cerulean exercise mat barefoot.

Head gear on, the friends became combatants. They exchanged strategic blows and grappled. Emma caught her opponent off guard with a powerful elbow to the abs. Sharp pain popped through Naomie's six pack and she released her submission hold. After feigning to distance herself, Naomie landed the winning blow. A butterfly kick twirled Emma around through the air and she smacked the mat spread eagled.

Naomie rushed to Emma's side to make sure she was okay, helping her up.

Emma tore her head gear off and babbled through her mouth guard. "According to KGW . . . The suspect . . . guard's gun . . . ditched the weapon. Another witness . . . comments section . . . described watching . . . stomped right up to Sarina Bassim. Her station . . . other side of the room."

Naomie feared that she'd hit her too hard. "Slow down, white girl. I don't understand a goddamn thing you're saying."

Emma yanked the mouth guard out. Blood and saliva dribbled down her chin. "Robbery wasn't the motive.

This son of bitch hates women, and I'm going to nail the fucker right to the wall."

●

Emma paid her debt in full at Genies Cafe on Division. In anticipation of a sore jaw and muscle aches, she ate a bowl of Bob's Red Mill oatmeal with banana slices and a dusting of cinnamon on top. Al Green was singing *Let's Stay Together* on the sound system. Naomie devoured a Florentine omelette, minus onions. Her fork clinked on the plate as she speared bites of fluffy egg, a trio of mushrooms, and spinach.

Emma sipped Stumptown java. A zing of citrus paired with notes of caramel and hazelnut soothed her tastebuds. Although she'd lost the fight, Emma was content in spending time with a friend and people watching. It fueled her craft. Cooing sounds at the table nearby got her attention.

A little boy in a booster seat opened his mouth wide as his mother lovingly fed him a small nibble of her Denver omelette. The adorable toddler gobbled it up. After making short work of the egg and cheddar, he smiled.

"Oh, you like that, huh. Okay, try this." Mom fed him a piece of green bell pepper.

The child spit it out and made a sour face.

A tender expression lightened Emma's spirits. The fuzzy feeling didn't last long, though.

Emma couldn't bear children. The rape had inflicted

too much damage. Her last boyfriend of more than a year abruptly broke up with her after she'd entrusted him with that reality on Halloween night.

She hadn't broken the bad news of the break up to Naomie yet. It wasn't an appropriate topic to bring up in a family restaurant. Emma knew Naomie would start dropping more F-bombs than Samuel L. Jackson in *Pulp Fiction*.

"That stuff you were carrying on about after I clobbered you," Naomie said, "what's it mean, or is it all *hush-hush*?"

Someone placing a mug on the formica table interrupted Emma before she could answer that question.

"Good morning, ladies," Glen said. "May I join you?"

It wasn't a question, not really. The cop was just being polite. He didn't wait for permission, and pulled up a chair to sit between them.

"Well . . ." Naomie said, scooping up the remnants of her scrumptious meal with the last piece of sourdough toast. "If it isn't the relative turned stalker."

"Hi, you must be Naomie. I'm glad my little cousin's got a tough friend to watch her back."

"I thought that was your responsibility," Naomie commented, persistent to pick a fight.

She chewed her last bite slowly, waiting for Glen to cross the line she'd drawn.

The professional didn't take the bait. When the waitress arrived to drop the check, Glen snatched it before Emma could. "Breakfast's on me."

"Thanks, Cuz." Emma smirked and nodded at Naomie sideways to ease up a bit.

"You're too kind," Naomie said.

She didn't mean it as a thank you to Glen. Naomie loathed cops. She was warning Emma not to be so nice to a person that may be trying to take advantage of her gifts. Tossing some cash on the table, Naomie stood up. Tilting his head upward slowly, Glen marveled at her height.

"I'll see you later, sugar," she said to Emma, then walked away.

Glen watched her leave. "I like her."

"Don't screw with me," Emma said. "I remembered Genies is one of your favorite breakfast diners, so I thought we could meet up and talk about the case."

"There's nothing to talk about," Glen said, hailing a waitress to order biscuits and sausage gravy, two eggs over easy on the side. "I've given you all you need, except the witness's contact information."

"Your note mentioned video surveillance was compromised. What about video from nearby businesses or street cameras?"

Glen nodded. "With the footage we were able to obtain, obstructions and pedestrians made identification unclear. And the suspect was too far away for enhancement to focus."

"How am I getting paid?" Emma said bluntly. "I doubt

my involvement has Commissioner Rose's blessing. If it did, the head of technology would be recruiting me. Not you."

"Your fee will come out of my own pocket," Glen guaranteed.

"Good, a girl's gotta eat," Emma said. "I've got some overdue bills to pay, and I could use a new TV."

"What happened to the one I got you last Christmas?"

"Never mind," she told him.

They sat in silence for a while. Emma finished off her porridge. The waitress topped off her coffee. Glen texted someone on his cell phone.

"Who's that?" Emma asked. "Is it related to Sarina Bassim?"

Glen scowled and paused to look up. "How do you know her last name?"

"Internet news search," Emma muttered behind the rim of the mug as she took a drink.

"Fine," he said. "Just do me a favor and don't even try to do more than you're being asked to here. Please . . ."

Emma drank her coffee and Glen continued to tap on his smartphone. There were moments where his fingers pressed hard with venom.

"Sweet," Glen said as his order arrived. The waitress warned the plate was hot. The detective pocketed his phone, then dug into the golden brown biscuits smothered in thick gravy. "I've arranged an appointment with you and the bank manger at his home. One of my detectives will also escort you there and stick around in case anything happens."

"Glen, I'm a grown woman and I can take care of myself."

Glen dissected the eggs and mixed the runny yolk in with the gravy. Shaking hot sauce on, he said, "My detectives are masterful at interviewing suspects. But when it comes to interacting with living victims or witnesses, they need to learn how to build a rapport."

"Enroll them in classes," she said. "That's where I learned."

Glen set the silverware down, a touch angry. "We both know that's BS. One of the things I regret the most was the time I missed spending with you and Jenny. She thoroughly trained you how to interview witnesses. While going through her stuff, I found a scrapbook Jenny built of all your forensic sketches next to the violent crime suspects they identified."

Emma spilled her coffee from the surprise. "I didn't know she did that."

"It's true," he said, picking the fork and knife back up to eat. "Besides, I think you'll like the detective I assigned. She used to be a cheerleader, like you."

"Ancient history," Emma said, dabbing the front of her shirt off with a napkin. "Did it ever occur to you that the suspect's motive wasn't money?"

"How's that?"

Emma grabbed a napkin from the dispenser. She asked Glen to draw a rough diagram of the bank floor and where the victim's station was. Glen frowned inwardly for not seeing this detail before.

"Why didn't he rob the teller closer to the entrance?" he asked, a bite of food sliding off the fork as he stared at the revelation, dismayed. The egg white rode Glen's paisley tie as it fell back on the plate, smearing yolk on the silk. He dabbed a napkin in his water glass and furiously scrubbed the fabric. "Dammit. This is brand new."

Silk accessories on a cop's budget weren't cheap. Emma wondered who Glen was trying to impress.

"I'm thinking Sarina Bassim was the real target," she said. "Maybe a lead in her apartment will reveal a reason why."

Glen nodded at the sound idea. He'd check out the victim's apartment that afternoon.

Emma stood up, put her thrashed jacket on to leave.

"Wait a sec, Emma." Glen wiped his hands and got up. "Turn around. This will drive me nuts all day thinking about if I don't fix it."

"What's bothering you now?"

"Just *turn* around."

"Okay, okay," Emma said, then felt Glen's fingers brushing the nape of her neck.

"There. That's better. The size tags on the back of your shirts were sticking out."

"They're supposed to, you idiot." She chuckled,

turning back around to give him a hug goodbye. "When is your detective picking me up and what's her name?"

"Heather MacGraw. She'll pick you up at 1500 hours," Glen told her. "And Emma, lose the punk clothes and wear something nice to the interview. You're representing the Portland Police Bureau."

She whispered gently in his ear. "Piss off."

SIX

The lady cop rolled up to the corner of Emma's apartment flat at Southeast Twenty-Seventh and Ash. She drove a sixties Mustang. From the moment Emma plopped down in the passenger's seat, Heather struggled to bridge the generation gap or find something mutual to talk about.

They drove by the Laurelhurst Theater. Heather pointed at the marquee that advertised *Bullitt* as now playing. The blonde pointed a thumb at the sign.

"I love that movie. My baby here is an exact replica of Steve McQueen's. You know, the one from the best car chase ever captured on film," she said, pridefully caressing the dashboard of her ride.

"Who's Steve McQueen?" Emma asked.

Heather's glossy peach lips formed an O. "You don't know the King of Cool. *The Magnificent Seven. The Great Escape. Papillon.*"

"What's that mean?" Emma said.

"It's French for 'butterfly,'" the detective said, making a leisurely right turn onto Sandy.

"Nope. I've never seen 'em. Sorry."

"Your loss," Heather said. "Try streaming them on Netflix sometime."

Emma shrugged and shook her head. "I don't watch a lot of old movies."

"We'll have to work on that," the cop said. "Maybe we can have a girls' night out. Take in a marathon and drink a brew."

A muscle car whipped out of the drive-thru at Wendy's. It pulled up alongside the Mustang. Gearheads with oil-stained faces and buzz cuts stared at Heather's glamorous looks. The cop sped up and left them behind. She cruised and strived to engage Emma in conversation.

"Glen told me you used to be a cheerleader," Heather said. "Where at?"

Where? More like when.

"It was another lifetime ago," Emma remarked in a 'I don't want to talk about it' tone.

They passed Gustav's Pub and Grill next to Der Rheinlander. Cozy place. Emma liked the warm apple cider there. The German restaurant was also the site of her third date with her now ex-boyfriend. They had made out in front of the weird, castle-like building on a cold night in December, embracing each other tight.

Heather tried talking about music.

"Listen, Detective. Enough with the small talk. I just want to interview the witness and sketch the suspect, alright. Aside from that, we have shit in common."

Although Portland was densely populated with goths, hippies, and punks, Heather admired Emma's singularity. It couldn't have been easy being raised by an older cousin whose sole purpose was climbing to the top of a police department's political hierarchy. Heather wanted to be a friend, but she understood that if Emma didn't want any of that, she needed to accept it.

Heather bit her lip and shifted gears to accelerate up the hill. "Fine by me. I'm not a babysitter."

Gazing at the detective through the corner of her eye, Emma considered if she might be a good person after all.

They arrived at the bank manager's residence on Wistaria. Stan Perry lived in a yellow Victorian house at the end of the street. The other houses that surrounded Perry's were either in disrepair or lacked landscaping to cut back the vegetation growing over the property. The front porch of the place next door was heaped with thrift shop goods marked "Free." Emma saw a crockpot that peaked her interest.

The two women got out of the car and walked up the steps to the door. They made quite an interesting duo. An athlete that never grew up beyond high school and an introverted glam punk.

Emma had ignored Glen's order to change her style for a reason. Next to Heather in her capris and U of O sweatshirt, she would've been overdressed. The advantage Emma took away from their 'non cop' appearances was a first impression that isolated Stan Perry's recollections from official police business.

Emma and Heather didn't look like cops, so maybe he'd relax enough to remember the face of Sarina

Bassim's attacker.

Heather rang the doorbell. Stan Perry greeted the women and welcomed them into his home. He didn't show any expression of being put off by their fashion sense. How could he? The banker was dressed down in jeans, a polo shirt, and loafers for a quiet Sunday. After the casual introductions were out of the way, Perry ushered them into the living room. Heather and Emma wiped their feet before following him inside.

Their blurred reflections were cast off from the polished oak floor. Oil paintings in ornate frames lined the walls. Emma didn't see a television. Shelves were stacked with books instead. An entertainment center housed a stereo system equipped with a turntable.

He dropped the needle on a record and a Wagnerian orchestra floated on the air in a whisper.

The heady aroma of bold coffee brewing wafted around the large room. Emma's senses buzzed as she inhaled.

Perry smiled in anticipation. "Can I pour either of you ladies a cup?"

Heather declined, but Emma chimed in with a yes. She didn't get the shakes from caffeine like most people do. The stimulant amplified her attention to detail.

They followed Perry into the kitchen. The surfaces gleamed, sterilized for a surgeon to operate on. After pouring two mugs of Joe and handing a bottle of mineral water to Heather, they sat down at the wooden prep table in the center of the room. Heather bumped her head on one of the pans hung up above.

"Ouch!" Perry said. "You okay detective? Do you need any ice?"

"No, I'm good. Thanks. Just clumsy sometimes."

"So," he said. "How do we begin? Should I start by talking about the events that led up to the attack?"

"No, no," the sketch artist said. "Drink your coffee and relax, Mr. Perry."

In Emma's experience, absolutes from a crime scene reconstruction were known to mislead or tamper with a witnesses memory.

"Please, call me Stan."

Emma slid an 8X10 tablet of drawing paper out of her bag. Next, she reached inside her jacket to produce a plain, number two wooden pencil and an ordinary pencil sharpener. Inserting the writing tip, she twisted it about seven times. Coiled shavings landed on the table.

Captivated, Perry looked on as Emma's red lips puckered up to blow on the pointy graphite tip. The words that came out of her luscious mouth melted the ice between her and the witness in a single breath.

"Tell me about yourself, Stan."

Emma tossed the simple line out like a talk show host interviewing a celebrity or a married couple renewing their fondness for each other on date night.

Perry talked about the paintings in the main room. He spoke of the countries he'd traveled to in order to obtain some of the pieces. One of the priceless works he recovered at a garage sale in a small, forgotten town not located on a map. He happened to be passing through on his way to the coast. Emma discovered that they shared a fondness for illustrations by Robert McGinnis.

She asked about the landmarks he'd encountered during his exciting travels. Perry elaborated that he marveled at the ancient structures in Greece. Emma injected a quick question. "Would you form a shape that's longer than wide or identical to length as width?"

The conversation moved to books. Perry owned an autographed copy of *The Thin Man*. He'd visited Ian Fleming's Goldeneye retreat in Jamaica where the James Bond novels were written. The banker donated money to local independent bookstores. He disliked e-books.

Perry refilled Emma's coffee and topped off his own.

Heather glanced around the spotless kitchen surfaces. The quickest path to a man's heart is through his stomach. Maybe that worked for memories, too.

"I take it you don't eat out a lot," she commented.

Emma nodded encouragement.

"No, I love cooking," Perry said, sitting back down. "It's wonderful being in control of what goes into my body."

They had a round table discussion about their favorite recipes. Heather licked her lips at hearing one for sweet potato lasagna. A dark molasses gingerbread cake made Emma's mouth water.

Perry mentioned that he preferred to use his hands when he cooked. The sketch artist saw a springboard and leapt. She referred to shapes and textures in their inanimate form, such as pliable substances like clay or dough, and asked how Perry would shape that substance into a face.

Emma engrossed Perry in subjects that he'd mastered. This focused the witness's mind for her to hone in on the abstract gallery of his darkest memories. Emma became a voice in Perry's imagination, guiding him through a maze. She diverted him from paths that lead to fear or terror. Emma didn't ask questions about the attack on Sarina. Such horrible details could upset Perry's emotions and allow his cognitive mind to assume control. Cognitive memory was most susceptible to influence and change. Emma didn't influence what Perry *thought* he saw.

Her hand drew across the paper, sketching the face he *actually* saw.

Prelude from *Parsifal* massaged Emma's nerves and loosened up her pencil strokes.

Sometime later, they adjourned to the living room. Rain was pinging the windows. Heather sat in a recliner, while Emma and Perry lounged on the opposite ends of a couch. The conversation went on. It allowed Emma to refine the suspect's features.

She took a photograph of the drawing and texted it to Glen.

He replied fast.

That's Sarina Bassim's ex-husband, Ahmed Bassim. A Salafi-jihad terrorist.

Heather's mobile bleeped and she answered it. "What?"

"Get your ass to the *Oregonian*," Glen said. "We might be able to get Emma's sketch published in time for the morning edition."

SEVEN

Reading glasses perched on his nose, Glen sifted through online sources to collect intel on Ahmed Bassim. To save the department some money on the utility bill, he'd turned the lights in his office off. The dim glow of the monitor lit up his scrolling eyes. He felt like he was on the bridge of a submarine. Glen clicked the mouse button aggressively for each site he looked at.

Ahmed Bassim came up in news reports that followed recent chemical attacks throughout Europe. The suspect attended Harvard in the nineties. He'd earned master degrees in biology, bioengineering, and nanotechnology. After 9/11, he fled the States. His name hadn't resurfaced until last year, when his ex-wife was granted asylum. Information she'd exchanged about the terrorists he associated with had warmed up cold trails on al-Qaeda sleeper cells all around the globe.

Glen's brow furrowed and his crow's feet became more pronounced. He wondered why Sarina Bassim hadn't been placed in round-the-clock witness protection. Furthermore, where had Ahmed gotten the financing to attend such a prestigious institution. All of that higher learning on a grant or scholarship just didn't seem to make sense. He wanted to know who had bankrolled

Ahmed Bassim's education. Maybe the Feds and the Patriot Act could be useful—for a change—and help him in access Ahmed's Harvard financial records.

He'd forwarded Emma's sketch to the FBI, but so far a "special agent" hadn't responded.

The cop thought back on the search he'd executed in Sarina Bassim's apartment while Emma interviewed Stan Perry. He'd gotten permission from her attorney. She lived in a modern townhouse near the Lloyd Center Mall. A tall gate surrounded the premises and motion-activated cameras covered the property in a digital mosquito net. An unarmed security guard patrolled the grounds day-and-night.

Even with latex gloves snapped on, Glen didn't handle many items. He preferred looking around to tearing things apart when he searched a victim's residence. A suspect's place, on the other hand . . . Well, it depended on if they were on scene and how hostile they got.

At Sarina Bassim's home, Glen had found items to propel the case forward rather quickly. He discovered a photo album in her bedroom. Most of the pictures with her and another individual were cut up to remove that person. Except one. It showed Sarina, a baby in her arms, and a lengthy man with chiseled, sun-baked features. They were standing by a man-made well under palm trees in an oasis. The man's remorseless eyes chilled Glen's blood. A picture hung on the refrigerator with magnets appeared to have been illustrated by a child.

Two stick figures and a car with tall buildings were drawn in crayon. Uneven block letters read, 'My new life with Mommy.'

Glen had asked the attorney about the identity of the man in the photograph, and Sarina's child. She had a little boy. As a part of her deal with the Justice Department, Sarina had been able to get his name changed. She'd enrolled him at the Alpha Omega Academy in Washington State. The Christian boarding school would be the last place where Ahmed Bassim, a Salafi-jihad terrorist, would look for his son.

Then Glen received the text from Emma. Pay dirt.

The detective loosened his silk tie and removed the glasses. As he leaned back, the old chair that'd belonged to his mentor and predecessor, Lou Mulgrew, creaked.

Glen felt a sense of accomplishment from knowing Ahmed's probable motive for the acid attack, but it didn't explain how he knew which bank Sarina worked at.

He picked up his cell phone to compare the picture of the oasis photo from Sarina's apartment with Emma's sketch again. Pride swelled in Glen's chest at how identical they were. She'd nailed the suspect's vicious gaze by coloring his eyes black as molasses.

Glen transferred seven hundred dollars to Emma's bank account. So what if he'd have to tighten his entertainment and grocery funds in his budget for a while.

With a guilty sigh, he looked at all the voicemail

notifications from his girlfriend. Glen realized the time and cursed. Tapping the playback button, he listened to the latest message.

"Where the hell are you, Glen? I've been sitting at the bar for over an hour. This is the second time you've stood me up for a dinner date. I understand you're a cop and that you're probably up to your eyeballs in work, but this isn't doing right by me. Goodbye, asshole."

He tossed the phone on his desk and sighed in frustration at himself. Sylvia was the first woman Glen had tried to have a steady, intimate relationship with since Jenny died three years earlier. He turned the monitor off and stretched out on the couch.

He nodded off. Ahmed Bassim's monstrous profile interrupted his REM cycle. The cop dreamt of pounding his face to a bloody pulp.

EIGHT

The land line ringing woke Glen up. He tumbled off the couch. Shaking his head, Glen got on his feet. His hands were sore from clenching his fists in his sleep. The dark wool slacks and blue dress shirt he'd slept in were wrinkled. He ambled over to his desk and picked up the phone. He glanced at the Venetian blinds. Daylight wasn't shining through the parted shades yet. It felt early. Three hours of sleep. Less.

Caffeine, he thought.

"Major Crimes. Captain Hart speaking."

"Captain, please don't put me on hold or transfer me someplace else!" a woman's muffled voice called out frantically.

The sound of panic delivered an urgent jolt through Glen's body.

"How can I help you, ma'am?"

"I'm calling about the picture in the paper," she said. "That man is living in my basement! All this time my husband and I thought we were just helping a hard-working refugee. But he's really al-Qaeda?"

Glen snatched a scrap of paper, knocked over a mug. Black coffee spilled out all over the desk. The cop didn't care and found something to write with.

"What's your name and address, please? Yes, I know where that is. It's in Laurelhurst. I'll be there in a few minutes. And Mrs. Jordan, don't do anything different than your normal morning routine. Try to act calm."

"Don't tell me to fucking act calm!" Angie Jordan shrilled. "Your kids haven't been playing in the park with a terrorist."

A child whined, "Mommy . . ."

Then the line clicked dead. He slammed the phone down.

"Shit!"

Glen snagged his shoulder holster off the coat rack and strapped it on, then stormed out of his office. At a few minutes till 6 A.M., the squad room was empty. Glen skidded to a stop as the right double door opened. Detective Walton was a south paw and opened the left side, balancing two pink boxes. Glen smelled bacon and maple.

"Morning, Cap," Walton said. "They gave us an extra dozen on the house."

Glen pulled on his junior detective's arm and the boxes fell. Frosted bars and glazed pastries littered the floor. "Screw the donuts," he said. "Let's go. I need some backup. We've got a positive I.D. and location on Ahmed Bassim. 3295 Southeast Ankeny Street."

Fruit Loop topping crunched beneath Walton's wingtips as he swung around and fell in alongside Glen, like a faithful shadow.

Glen and Walton pounded along the sidewalk. Glen's right foot dragged. Thunder crackled overhead. They jumped into Glen's unmarked gray Dodge Charger. Glen plugged his Android in the dock on the console. Revving the engine on, he gunned the sedan away from the curb.

First, the detectives needed to cross the Willamette River.

A dozen motor vehicles and bicyclists were waiting in line for the Hawthorne Bridge. Lights on the truss were flashing. It's vertical lift was raised. The horn of a tugboat wailing drowned out Glen's curses.

He veered North onto Naito Parkway. A motorist he cut off screeched to a halt and leaned on their horn. The stench of burnt rubber tainted the air. Glen threaded a needle through traffic.

Walton swallowed his fear in a dry gulp and wobbled side-to-side. He fastened his seatbelt and tightened it snug.

Glen eased his foot off the gas. The sea of taillights up ahead was getting crowded. Red and white bokeh balls expanded into focus through the windshield. They weren't going to make the Burnside Bridge quick enough and the Morrison Bridge had recently closed for repairs.

"Maybe we can take a detour to the Steele Bridge," the younger cop suggested.

Except for a row of orange sawhorses topped with whirling caution lights, the exit ramp for Morrison beckoned to Glen's desperate instincts.

"Hold on," he said and floored the accelerator, swerving hard over to the left.

"*Cap* . . .!" Walton yelled, arms braced on the dashboard.

The Charger smashed through the barricade. Glen whipped round the curve. The speedometer needle reached fifty and kept climbing.

Centrifugal force mashed Walton's right cheek and shoulder into the window. "This a bad idea," he mumbled.

Bright headlights pierced thick patches of fog and illuminated obstacles ahead. Glen altered course at the last second. Walton flinched as the passenger side mirror snapped clean off. The Charger sheered a stack of rebar underneath a reflective blue tarp. A dull scraping sound grated his nerves.

Walton's eyes widened and all he could do was point.

"I see it," Glen said nonchalantly, turning the wheel a fraction of an inch to the right.

He steered around a two car-length gap carved out of the concrete in the left lane. The rear bumper nudged a tool chest and knocked it over into the void. The chest of drawers hit the tributary below with a heavy splash.

They were barreling toward a pair of oncoming forklift tongs. The Dodge's high beams lit up a construction worker's shocked expression. Glen braked and swerved around the utility vehicle. Tires scorched the asphalt with tread marks. The construction worker yelled profanity and called them lunatics.

The Charger breached the east side barricade. A wooden sign cracked in half and peppered the windshield with splinters. Glen sped left onto Grand Avenue. A hubcap popped off and rolled along the street. He weaved around cars that obstructed his path.

Glen breathed a sigh of accomplishment, speeding east along Burnside. Maybe he beat a time record. He glanced at Walton. The younger detective's complexion was turning a sick shade of pale.

"You still with me, Walton? Open the window if you have to throw up."

"Christ, Cap, where'd you learn to drive?"

"Logging roads," Glen said.

His smartphone vibrated and flashed a call from a contact named G-Man.

"Who's that?" Walton asked.

"Special Agent Olivia Burrows."

"Want me to answer it?"

"The Feds can go pound sand," Glen said. "We're a little busy right now."

They rocketed past Union Jacks, a strip joint mainstay. A patrol car pulled out from a nearby corner and gave pursuit, sirens howling.

"What you can do is call dispatch though," Glen said, "and get that Crown Victoria off our backs. I don't want Ahmed Bassim spooked into running."

Walton dug his cell out of his side pocket and phoned dispatch. He rattled off his badge number and relayed his captain's orders. The sirens stopped and the blue-on-white Ford careened right onto Twenty-Eighth Avenue.

Two blocks south of Music Millennium, then turning east at the Bridgetown Church, Glen prowled Ankeny Street. Square bell towers of bleached granite bordered the worshipping place's entrance. The terrain was flat. Property tax aside, the prices of the luxury homes in the upscale neighborhood cost more money than Glen would ever make in his lifetime.

A group of twenty-something bicyclists pedaled out of a driveway and zipped by in the opposite direction. The riders weren't wearing helmets or proper reflectors. The privileged yuppies probably thought they were immortal. They were totally oblivious to the possibility of a terrorist threat hiding out in their suburban paradise.

Portland prided itself on art, coffee, E-commerce, and microbrews. Ordinary people indulged simple pleasures. These weren't exactly prime targets catalogued under the rule book of international terrorism.

That's how it made it so easy for an al-Qaeda agent to hide in plain sight.

Until throwing acid in his ex-wife's face, Ahmed Bassim probably acted just like any other tourist on holiday, or refugee looking to rebuild a plain, everyday life.

In addition to the suspect's background in chemical

engineering weighing heavily on his mind, a nasty thought was beginning to boil in Glen's gut. He needed to find out what other recreational activities Ahmed Bassim pursued.

Angie Jordan's fearful voice echoed inside his head.

'Your kids haven't been playing in the park with a terrorist.'

The detectives urgently scrutinized house numbers.

Glen hadn't bothered to turn on the heater, and the temperature outside was dipping in the low forties. Although he didn't feel ill, Glen was running hot. Beads of sweat were forming along his receding hairline.

Even cops got scared.

If a massive coronary hadn't killed Lou before his time, he would've taunted Glen just then.

Man up, Hart. No one lives forever.

Glen's mentor boosted his courage in other ways than memories of heroic sentiment.

Taking a deep breath, Walton pointed to the left at Thirty-Third Avenue.

"There it is, Cap. 3295."

Smoke plumed from the chimney. Notes of cedar in the air conjured up a peaceful mood. In the east end of the backyard a medium-sized Douglas Fir, it's leaves and branches swaying in a strong wind, sentineled the two-story, Colonial-style edifice.

An elderly man with a jaunty spring in his step bounced down the stairs. His starched white button-down shirt and creased slacks were a bright contrast to the flower gardens of hibernating plants that flanked the cement walkway. He wore a black satin bow tie and a white dress hat tilted up high on his forehead that read 'Moo' in red letters above a black patent leather visor.

Just another beautiful morning delivering nature's perfect, wholesome food to families about to start their day.

Glen parked across the street. As the snub-nosed delivery truck pulled away from the curb, the detectives jogged up to the door. A gust of wind blew a whirlwind of leaves in their path. They reached the porch. Glen happened to glance down at the four half-gallon bottles of milk in a carrier. The dairy marked the silver caps with silhouettes of which plant or species the milk came from: An almond, a cow, a goat, and a sheep.

The deadbolt clicked and the thick English oak door opened. Both cops placed a hand on their sidearms.

They glimpsed a pair of toned calves through a rustling blue velvet robe. The long legs led up to a lithe blonde holding a toddler in one arm, while she cradled a cell phone up to her ear. Her eyes fixed to the shields clipped on the front of the detective's belts.

"Gotta' go," Angie Jordan said. "Cops just got here."

Glen recognized her voice from the phone.

"Who's that you're speaking with, Mrs. Jordan?" he said.

"My husband," she said. "He's a firefighter. He'll be

home in about thirty minutes."

Terrific, Glen thought, *just what we need.*

A fireman confronting a terrorist in his house. That could significantly escalate the threat of rash impulses in this situation. His own blood was up enough.

Glen *hated* abusive men. He never forgave himself for ignoring his instincts, and not going after the animals that had raped Emma ten years ago. Then he really screwed up when the county laid her off and he didn't go to bat for her about how vital her skill set was in nailing suspects.

He saw his second chance to make things right.

"Mrs. Jordan," Glen said, "I don't want you or your family in harm's way. Is there a neighbor's house nearby you can stay at? Maybe you can tell them your power's out and you're waiting for your husband to arrive to find and replace the fuse."

The housewife shook her head no. The pointed ends of Angie Jordan's blonde bob flipped about her Nordic features and accentuated her full, stern lips.

"My neighbors think I'm a whore," she said, her brown doe eyes crossed with anger. "They don't like how I make a living as a pole dance instructor."

The toddler pulled his thumb out of his mouth. "Fuck, fuck, fuck—"

He'd heard his mommy curse while they were eating breakfast.

Angie Jordan cupped a hand over her son's mouth.

He giggled and squirmed playfully.

"Come in," she said, keeping her voice calm and level. "I want that man out of my house."

The detectives stepped inside the foyer. Walton picked up the carrier full of milk and set it down on a small square table next to a short stack of mail that included a lingerie catalogue. A photograph in an ornate frame showed a little boy and a girl riding ponies at the fair.

"Where are your other children?" he said.

"Feverish in their beds upstairs, and complaining about my oatmeal being too lumpy."

Glen peered down the narrow flight of stairs to the left of the foyer. "Why don't you join them, please. Watch some cartoons. Anything to try and keep your mind occupied."

Angie Jordan nodded.

"Detective Walton," continued Glen. "Guard the stairs. If I don't text you in ten minutes that the suspect's in custody, call for backup. Understand?"

"Shouldn't we take him together, Cap?"

Glen squeezed Walton's shoulder assuringly. "I need you to protect the family."

"You got it, Captain."

"Mrs. Jordan," Glen said and pointed at the bottles of goat and sheeps milk. "Are these his?"

"Yes."

"Does he come upstairs to get his milk, or do your

kids take the bottles down?"

"My daughter sets them by the basement door and knocks."

"Okay, thank you. Detective Walton, escort Mrs. Jordan. Stay alert."

Glen watched them walk through the living room past a Steinway and the crackling fireplace. The flickering embers cast a devilish aura in the dim atmosphere.

He kicked his shoes off. Drawing his service weapon with one hand and holding the milk carrier in the other (sans the almond and cow juices), Glen crept down the stairs on the balls of his feet. He distributed his weight lightly to mimic a child's footsteps. Halfway down, a warped board creaked. He heard a man's voice behind the door clear his throat. Glen froze and raised his Glock 17. He shut an eye and zeroed in on the peephole through the gun's sight.

Past the last steps, Glen set the carrier down by the door, then put his back to the left wall. It was a sloppy attempt to stay out of the view through the peephole. He rapped lightly on the door three times. Sweat was dripping down his temples and goosebumps dotted his bare forearms.

The seconds it took for the occupant to answer dragged Glen through the longest moment of his entire life.

Maybe Angie Jordan's daughter always delivered with a greeting. Maybe complacency was a disadvantage on Glen's side. Perhaps Ahmed Bassim had grown so accustomed to the innocence and warmth of his hideout that he didn't bother checking the peephole anymore.

The door unlocked and opened wide enough for an olive-skinned hand to reach down for the bottles. The flesh was calloused and weathered, but the nails were immaculately trimmed. Long fingers curled around the handle and stopped.

Glen's gut started to fathom his one mistake.

He didn't take the bottles out of the carrier.

The hand withdrew.

Kicking the door in, Glen rammed the surface with every pound of muscle he possessed behind his shoulder. The brutal sneak attack caught the man inside off guard. He grunted in pain. The plywood door smacking his face and splitting his lip were the least of his problems.

As Ahmed Bassim's black doll eyes looked up from the hardwood floor, watery from the jarring impact, his forehead collided with the end of a cold steel tube.

Glen pressed the gun barrel hard against the center of Bassim's forehead.

"Good morning from the Portland Police Bureau, asshole."

Stunned, Bassim's dark eyes rolled around to focus, while blood dribbled down his chin.

"How did you find me?" he asked.

His index finger rigid alongside the trigger guard, the cop applied more pressure to the muzzle stamp.

Bassim's skin dimpled.

"The old fashioned way," Glen said. "A forensic sketch on the front page of the newspaper. Put your hands on your head, interlace your fingers."

A smug grin tugged at the corner of Bassim's mouth. He followed the detective's commands.

Glen took one hand off the pistol butt and reached inside his rear trouser pocket. Empty. He'd forgotten his handcuffs. He nudged Bassim an inch back with the Glock.

"Turn around," he ordered the terrorist. "Move toward that wall."

The detective and his prisoner walked between a cozy living room and a kitchenette that included a stove, a dishwasher, and a compact refrigerator. The finished quarters featured amenities such as a plush beige loveseat, a coffee table carved out of American walnut, and a big screen television complete with a cable box. A layer of dust covered the TV set. In the corner, Glen saw an ugly coat rack with a jacket and beanie draped over it. The rack resembled a wooden man.

Every burner on the glass range was occupied. Two medium-sized pots were covered and simmering. A large teakettle sat on top of a glowing element. The rich aroma of Turkish coffee brewed in a decorative copper tin almost masked the pungent odor of what Ahmed Bassim was really concocting.

The common household chemicals and a bottle of

corn syrup on the counter dredged up a case the detective fought to repress.

Five years ago, a joint task force of the BATF, area detectives, and the Grunge Operatives raided an extremist group headquartered in an abandoned hotel near the airport. They were targeting innocent Muslim citizens on holiday. Along with the illegal firearms they seized, Glen and the agents had interrupted an assembly line of runaway teenagers (one of them a lost girl a judge hired Matt and Leslie to find) putting together crude pipe bombs.

He'd never forget their brainwashed faces or that smell.

Ahmed Bassim was cooking up nitroglycerin.

Glen noticed a cerulean blue rubber mat laid out across the floor between the entertainment center and the table.

"Those are nice silk sweatpants you're wearing," Glen said. "They must be expensive. Poor choice for concealed weapons." He approved. "I don't care for the skulls though. Are they comfortable to pray in?"

"I practice yoga, Captain Hart. It keeps my body toned and my mind sharp."

"Hold it, dickhead. How do you know my name?"

Glen saw the terrorist's smirk reflected in the TV screen.

"I must've read about you in the newspaper." Bassim mocked.

The detective cocked an eye at the reflection. A vest hung from a hook on the back of the basement door. Glen couldn't believe he'd neglected to check the corner like a rookie.

"Unless you want to eat a bullet," he said, "don't move a *fucking* muscle."

Keeping the terrorist covered with his pistol, Glen shuffled over to the door. He took a pencil out of his pocket, then carefully lifted the frayed denim vest off the hook. By the retro design and the cut of the fabric he could tell the thrift store apparel belonged on a woman.

The size on the tag indicated an 'S'. Emma wore a small. The detective didn't believe in coincidences. He was beginning to fear if a search of the bedroom in the foyer off the kitchen would reveal surveillance photos of his cousin tacked to the walls.

Glen tossed the garment on the coffee table, then slipped the pencil in his pocket. He pulled himself together. Lots of girls liked to wear grungy clothes these days. "Who were you making an explosive vest for?"

"I'm not going to surrender my agenda that easily, Captain."

"Actually," Glen mulled over as he walked back toward Bassim, and dug his phone out of his pocket to text Walton. "I'm hoping you'll resist arrest so I can beat the shit out of you. Just a little. Yeah, I'd really enjoy that. You have the right to remain silent—"

The kettle whistled. Glen twitched and turned his

head for a brief second.

Spinning around counter-clockwise, Bassim delivered a shocking roundhouse kick. Glen's sidearm went sailing across the room. The Glock hit the wall and fell down behind the futon. He tilted sideways to give his opponent less to strike at, and raised his forearms to block. His right arm parried a vicious left hook. Blunt force trauma pounded his muscles and bones.

The combination he was suspecting in a follow up right hook stopped short. Instead, Glen's vantage point tilted upward and gravity smashed him downward as Bassim swept the detective's legs right out from beneath him. He landed on his tailbone. Before he could wince in pain, Glen saw the bottom of Bassim's foot stomping down at his nose.

Glen rolled sideways and got up to one knee. Bassim launched a rapid front kick at Glen's stomach. The detective caught the terrorist's calve. He felt two ferocious jabs pound his jaw. Blood flooded Glen's mouth. While the detective was dazed, Bassim used his own leverage against him. He jumped up and kicked the side of Glen's head in.

The detective's solid grip hung on though. Both men tumbled into the entertainment center. Their momentum knocked the cart over. The TV set fell. The screen cracked and the picture tube shot sparks through its back.

Bassim rolled backward into a squatting position. He drove an uppercut into Glen's chin. The detective reeled sideways where his head struck the cupboards underneath the sink. Reaching up, Glen clawed the edge of the counter. The battered muscles in his arms gave out. He bellyflopped onto the floor and wheezed, the wind knocked out of his body.

Although Bassim was a foot shorter than Glen, he towered over the beaten detective. He opened the fridge, reached inside, then kicked the door shut. He held a baby food jar that contained a clear liquid.

"I could pour this acid on you, Captain Hart," the terrorist said, "but I'd rather you live the rest of your life with the failure of stopping me. I'm certain your partner will break as easy as you have." He walked away, heading for the door. "I wonder if Angie Jordan will scream as loud as my ex-wife after I repay her hospitality."

Glen spit out his response. "Here's my partner."

Bassim turned back around to give the detective a parting smirk.

The gunshot roared in the close quarter confines of the basement. Bassim saw a quick tongue of flame lick the air like the devil. A terrible pain enveloped the terrorist's groin and the short range impact slammed his backbone into the wall. He screamed soprano.

"Did she sound anything like that?" Glen shouted.

The detective's eyes squinted to see through the smoke drifting up from the barrel of his mentor's revolver. Lou had bequeathed his Chief's Special to 'the finest and toughest policeman he'd ever trained'. Glen carried the .38 Smith & Wesson loaded with hollow-point bullets as a backup strapped to his ankle.

Ahmed Bassim continued to scream in agony, clenching the shredded meat of his crotch that used to be genitals. Blood ran in rivulets down his thighs. The slug had expanded to rip more tissue apart for a maximized wounding effect.

Glen savored the sound he'd wanted to hear for a decade. The system had failed to administer justice to Emma's rapists. For now, the high-pitched screaming of an abusive husband popped in his ears like fireworks. As he heard Walton's voice call out at the top of the stairs, Glen squeezed the trigger again.

The terrorist's head jerked backward in a *coup de grâce* of skull fragments and brain matter that splattered the bricks.

A sharp pain tightened Glen's skull in a vice grip. The gun slipped through his loosening fingers, and his focus on the blood faded to black as he lost consciousness.

NINE

Emma gasped in short terrified bursts. The weight of a muscular teenage boy was pressing down on top of her. The stench of cheap beer overwhelmed Emma with sour hops. The oxygen the rapist burned through to maintain the momentum of his tearing thrusts came out in grunts like an animal.

"Oh God, please don't," Emma screamed until her voice cracked. Tears gushed down her cheeks. "No . . . Stop it! *Pleeeease* . . . Get off me," she shrieked. "NO . . ."

She thrashed about.

Large hands wrapped around Emma's throat and applied just enough pressure to incapacitate the fight in her. She couldn't get any air and tried to clutch her throat, but one of the accomplices had restrained her wrists above her head. His giant ring indented her skin. A third guy held onto her ankles.

"That's right. Fight back, *whore*," the leader panted. "Oh shit, yeah! Here . . . I . . . *Come!*" His face collapsed on top of Emma's. He drooled on her.

Emma's body spasmed violently. The semen pumped inside her like a disgusting slime.

The length of torture she suffered went on forever. Emma felt like she'd been fucked by a locomotive. Her sniffles receded. Shock set in.

"Do you think we're finished!" he yelled. "Turn her over. Where's her spirit stick trophy? Spread her legs wider, Jake."

"No names," the college-bound quarterback said.

"She's drugged," the leader argued. "Bitch will be lucky to remember her own name. What are you worried about anyway, rich boy? Your alibi is solid. Oh, wait . . . I get it. You want your turn, only you don't want to look her in the face. Well giddy up! Get your goddamn hands off me."

Sounds of their brawling echoed in the woods. Knuckles pounded flesh and bone. The hands securing her wrists released her. Something heavy whooshed through the air. Wood splinters were crushed. Another swing drove a yelp out of Jake.

Emma ripped the bandanna off. She saw the Confederate Flag pattern on the fabric clearly. There were cursive initials embroidered on it, too. Twigs scratched the bottoms of her feet or snapped as Emma sprinted into the dense foliage. The bright headlights on the pickup she'd been abducted in lit a path through the evergreens.

Until the silhouette of a man holding a gun stepped out from behind a Douglas Fir to block her escape. He raised the weapon, aimed the barrel at her face. A muzzle flash flared.

●

Eyes opening wide from the nightmare, Emma jackknifed into a sitting position.

The abrupt movement shook the full-sized mattress and the box spring slammed the headboard against the wall. Arms flailing, she knocked an 8X10 photograph of Jenny off the nightstand. The corner of the wood frame hit the floor on a corner and the pane cracked into slivers.

After taking a minute to catch her breath, Emma lunged out from underneath the duvet. She rummaged through the basket of clean clothes near the hamper at the foot of the bed. Pulling out a pair of panties, she gave up scrounging in the dark for other fresh garments, and grabbed a dirty tank top and flannel shirt off the shag carpet. Emma put on the musty clothes.

An aluminum baseball bat rolled out of the way. She winced at the broken monitor of the TV set on top of the dresser.

The night she'd told Glen that she'd take the case and sketch the profile, Emma's long work day ended snuggling with her body pillow, warming up to a mug of tomato soup and a toasted cheese sandwich. She turned the television on for noise while she ate and caught up on some blogs and social media posts. Leno came on. Emma actually chuckled at a few jokes in his monologue.

Then Leno's first guest walked out on stage wearing an old football jersey from his high school football team. Jake waved at the cheering crowd, slapped the talk show host's hands with a high five. Emma noticed how most of the whistles and lustful screams were women.

If only they knew the truth. Jake Warren was a sexual sadist.

He took a seat on the end of the couch near Leno's desk. They chatted about Jake's football career ending early due to a cartilage injury in his knee, then moved on to his hobby of financing independent horror films, which garnered the attention of Hollywood.

"You're in pre-production for your next movie right now, aren't you?" Leno asked.

"Yes, I am," Jake commented. "It's going to be a murder mystery based on a real case in my hometown. I'm really excited about taking the private eye genre and turning it on its head."

"How are you going to do that, exactly?" Leno said.

"Well, the main characters are based on the true crime private eyes that investigated the murders. You probably know them as the Grunge Operatives. Imagine if Kurt Cobain was a detective instead of a rock star, and his partner was a sexy, urban Native American woman."

"No," the talk show host said, "I can't say I've heard of them before."

"Don't worry," Jake said. "After my movie breaks box office records, you will. You will. I might not be a football star anymore, but I still know how to chase my goals down like I'm running for a touchdown."

He toasted the audience with his cup of coffee. Their loud cheers reminded Emma of the fireworks that went off at Homecoming the night she'd been assaulted. The date-rape cocktail that'd been slipped into her diet soda amplified her senses before rendering a paralyzing effect and inflicting retrograde amnesia. One sip enabled Jake to carry Emma to his truck, dump her in the back, then drive off to the secluded clearing.

The murder case Jake mentioned had overshadowed the investigation into her rape, and a fire the killer ignited at the crime lab to kill Matt Grudge and Leslie Crow destroyed evidence.

Emma screamed with rage and swung the bat into the screen. Shards flew and got tangled up in her hair. Exhausted, she dropped the slugger.

"I've been wanting to upgrade to a flatscreen, anyway," she'd muttered, then cried herself to sleep.

Emma had shed her last tears for the trauma she'd gone through that night.

Driven to render the new clue from her memories, Emma hustled into the living room of her one-bedroom flat. A tall bookcase crammed with assorted drawing tablets and essential texts on drawing human anatomy, along with Emma's drafting table, occupied the corner near the archway to the kitchen. She snatched a leather bound volume from a high shelf, then hopped up onto the stool at the slanted desk.

As Emma leaned forward, her butt cheeks pressed into the freezing cushion. She opened the large sketchbook's patinated cover. The image she'd drawn in charcoal and graphite on the first page ten years ago represented the forest she'd ran through to escape. Emma leafed through a few more pages and gazed upon the owl she'd heard, and caught a glimpse of, looking over her shoulder for Jake or his accomplices in pursuit.

Emma recollected Leslie Crow's sage remarks when she'd shared the illustrations with the P.I. To some American Indian nations the owl signified death approaching, while other tribes viewed the nocturnal bird as a protective guardian for brave warriors. It's huge, forward-facing eyes still ruffled the hairs on the nape of Emma's neck.

She flipped through a few more sketches. The massive lights on the Hellberg's semi truck glared through driving rain. Emma's muddied and scraped arms outstretched from the bottom of the page waved stop.

Three-quarters into the tablet, Emma came across a blank page and started drawing.

Fluid strokes defined the shape of the blindfold. Emma added her broken nails pulling the left side of the bandanna up. Vertical swipes defined tree branches and a ray of light from Jake's pickup illuminating the cursive script embroidered on the cotton.

R.C.W.

The timer on the coffeemaker beeped and brew streamed. Emma inhaled the dark roast. It fueled her craft.

Once she completed the overall outline, Emma

smeared charcoal with her thumbs. The shading added a layer of gritty depth that brought out the wrinkles in the handkerchief. She blurred the trees. Emma needed people to see that although escape was at her fingertips, freedom had never seemed so far away.

She could've just scrawled the initials down on a piece of scratch paper. That would've been tantamount to Leonardo da Vinci painting nothing else but Lisa del Giocondo's smile on the *Mona Lisa*.

Besides, Emma lived as an artist; she'd fight and die as an artist, too.

Scrawling her signature along the bottom right corner, Emma took a picture of the piece with her smartphone. She swiveled around and stretched. The vertebrae in her spine popped. Emma stood up to move into the kitchen, then poured a cup of black java.

She parted the blinds by the back door and dining room table. Sunlight made her blink in disbelief. Emma tilted her head up at the blue sky. She sipped coffee, then checked the weather app on her cell phone. Strangely enough, the forecast called for the day's temperature to hover in the low seventies. Emma reminded herself it was early November. She'd take it. Especially since she planned on paying a visit to the cemetery later on.

Her stomach rumbled. Emma opened the refrigerator and searched the poorly-stocked shelves for breakfast. Saliva oozed from her glands at the site of two eggs and the wild mushrooms Izabella and Amanda had foraged while on a geocaching expedition. Izabella gifted them to Emma last week after life modeling for her art class. The mushrooms sautéed in butter with a fragrant clove of minced garlic. She added the whisked eggs, then topped the golden scramble with a handful of shredded mozzarella.

Emma took a seat at the table. After twisting the pepper mill a couple times, she dug in. The savory food melted in her mouth. She checked her e-mail. When Emma opened the message from her bank and she saw the transfer from Glen, a bite of egg went down her windpipe. Coughing and gagging, she dropped her fork and handset to rush over to the sink for a glass of water.

Between the clue in the initials from her bad dream, the payment for Bassim's portrait, and the cash she'd saved up over the last couple months, Emma wanted to hire Matt and Leslie to find Jake Warren's accomplices.

Yes, she understood that the statute of limitations (an appallingly-short six-year limit) would insulate the criminals from prosecution. Emma believed that she'd earned the right to know the identities of *all* her attackers. Furthermore, she was dedicated to stopping them from raping other girls.

The Alternative Investigations operatives also owed her for the consultation she'd begun with an exotic dancer to identify the odious face of a black market surgeon. Trixie had seen him the night one of her co-workers was killed, and Matt got his ass kicked by a deadly mercenary.

The private eyes sought him in connection with a money laundering setup at the Ardor strip club.

Emma set the dishes in the sink to soak. Trotting off to the bathroom, she cleaned up nicely. A touch of makeup accentuated the beauty of her pale features.

Returning to the bedroom, Emma put on something cool for the uncharacteristically nice, warm day. A black tank top, denim cutoffs, and a sleeveless, studded vest would turn some heads to the pastel tattoo sleeve on her left arm, or the full-color wolf's face inked on her chest. Black floral nylons with well-worn combat boots offset the elegance of her magnificent gams. Long red hair lit Emma's glam punk persona on fire.

She slung her brown canvas rucksack over her shoulder, then headed for the back door and stopped. Emma turned her head slightly. The smell of breakfast lingered. A sense of accomplishment buzzed in her brain. She couldn't remember the last early morning that'd turned out so good. Opening the door, Emma crossed the threshold, and left her apartment.

Curry hung in the air. Emma didn't care much for Indian-style cuisine. She blamed the stench on the dumpster nearby.

Keys in hand, Emma walked to her car parked around the corner on Ash. She began to smile at a little girl drawing flowers on the sidewalk. Then her lips pursed to silence bad language in front of the kid.

The tires were slashed. She decided to deal with the

repairs later and kept walking.

At the northeast corner of Twenty-Eighth and Burnside, Emma waited for a bus to take her downtown. The subtle notes of maple and pumpkin spice emanating from Starbucks eliminated the curry smell. Traffic pulled over for an ambulance, three police cruisers, and a bomb squad truck hauling ass, east. She saw the convoy turn right past Music Millennium.

●

Emma stepped off the bus at Northwest Fifth Avenue. She crossed the four lanes of Burnside. A fuel attendant at Chevron singled Emma out in the cosmopolitan metropolis and couldn't help but stare. He failed three times to hook the nozzle back into the pump.

Emma's footsteps through the bus mall quickened.

She passed the food carts that occupied half the lot between Oak and Stark Street. Vendors were hustling to get ready for the imminent lunch rush. The independent businesses catered a diversity of foods; from Chinese to Thai or Czechoslovakian to Italian. And of course, Indian. Emma thought their cute chef bore a slight resemblance to Billy Zane. *Demon Knight* was one of her favorite scary movies. He'd flirted with Trixie and gave her his number.

The cook had tried to charm Emma too, but she wasn't there to hook up. And he reeked of curry.

The private detectives had set up Emma's first meeting with Trixie at the food carts a few weeks back. She didn't blame the stripper's reluctance to be a witness. A terrible scar she described on the black market doctor's right cheek stoked her fear. The exotic dancer picking at her Szechuan orange chicken and noodles had indicated the topic also upset her appetite. The forensic sketch artist had chipped away at the ice by talking about music they had in common. An appreciation for Björk pulled Leslie into the conversation, and helped Trixie relax. Then the stripper got called into work early. Emma looked forward meeting with her again. Trixie was interested in filling in as a life model in Emma's art class while Izabella traveled abroad on her winter holiday.

Emma yanked the glass door open and entered the Kress Building. As she jogged up to the second floor, the soles of her boots stomping steps echoed up the stairwell. She turned the knob to the outer office door of Alternative Investigations.

It was locked.

Emma knocked on the frosted glass between the stenciled operative names *Matt Grudge & Leslie Crow*. She checked her phone. The time read a few minutes past 10 A.M. No one answered.

She dialed their business number.

"You've reached the offices of Alternative Investigations. Please leave your name and phone number after the beep," Matt's voicemail greeting said. "We'll call you back."

"No, no, no," Emma rattled off. "Don't be out of

town. Not now."

She shot Leslie a text.

> Urgent. Break in my rape case. New lead to follow. Must meet to hire you.

The cooler down the hall gurgling startled her. Emma poured a cup of water. She sat down in one of the chairs that bookended the cooler, and waited for a while. To pass the time, Emma played a few rounds of Fruit Ninja.

A warm breeze above her head started to blow. The air vent emitted a rattling sound. She smelled curry again and her face crinkled up in bewilderment. Emma peaked in the waist basket by the cooler, only to find it empty. She crushed her paper cup and tossed it in the trash. Someone in a neighboring suite had probably ordered Indian for lunch and a fan in the ducts was carrying the spices.

Emma tapped out a news search on Google. The key words were: Portland, Oregon, Bassim, and Fugitive. The stairwell door opened, and the sight of a familiar face curved Emma's lips into a genuine smile. She turned her head away from the palm-sized screen that went to sleep.

"Thanks again for the mushrooms," Emma said. "They were very tasty."

"You're welcome," Izabella Sommer replied in her

husky voice, heading for Alternative Investigations.

The sketch artist got up and joined the androgynous model. Emma admired her hair. Izabella had put her coarse locks up into a mohawk that must've required at minimum two cans of hairspray to hold in place.

"They're out," Emma said in a helpful tone.

Izabella's knuckles stopped mid-knock. "Oh. Any idea when they'll be back?"

"I texted Leslie almost an hour ago. She hasn't gotten back to me yet, which isn't like her at all. It's not what I need today. Some asshole already slashed my tires, and now I can't hire them to help me check a new lead."

"Don't fret, Emma. Matt and Leslie might be on a surveillance job, or in a meeting."

Emma nodded at the comforting words. Izabella was right. "I've gotta' tell you. My students draw their best portraits during your sessions."

"That's a nice thing to hear." Izabella smiled in return. A few heartbeats later her cell phone sounded a text alert. "Excuse me a moment."

While Izabella read her message, Emma grabbed her bag from beside the chair.

"I've got a suicide cleanup job out near Oregon City, Emma. Need a lift to the cemetery? I can pick you up when I'm done and take you home."

TEN

They made a couple of pit stops in route to their destinations. Izabella steered the panel truck into a gas station near the old bomber in Milwaukie. After filling up the tank, she parked in the lot. Beyond a small field to the west, an apartment complex and a mobile home park stood nestled in the trees. The Hellbergs used to live in that retirement community. Autumn had colored the leaves orange and red. Dark storm clouds were rolling in from the west. Every now and then an electrical charge pulsed inside the puffy mass.

Reaching behind the driver's seat, Izabella pulled a backpack around and into her lap.

"I need to fix my hair," she said, then pointed. "See those apartments? A woman about our age was strangled there a little over a year ago. I cleaned the unit after the Bureau released the property back to the landlord. The killers had painted runes in chicken blood all over the victim's bedroom walls. Christ, what a mess."

"I don't know how you stomach being a biohazard cleaner," Emma said.

"Pays good. And it helps afford the timeshare Amanda and I vacation at every year," Izabella said, then hopped down from the cab.

Emma watched Izabella in the rear view mirror strut back to the kiosk. She got the key attached to a block of wood from the attendant and ducked into the bathroom. For her friend's sake, Emma hoped the facility was clean on the inside. Gang tags and oil stains streaked the door.

Emma tried hard not to stare at the apartments Izabella had referred to. Images of the grizzly, ritualistic murder were beginning to take shape in her imagination. She took a deep cleansing breath when Izabella returned about thirty minutes later. Her funky dreads were back too.

A few miles up McLoughlin Emma asked to stop at the Oak Grove Fred Meyer. She picked up two bouquets, and treated Izabella to lunch in the deli. Emma ordered a roasted turkey wrap with cranberry sauce and cream cheese, while Izabella preferred a ham sandwich on dill rye. They shared a side of carrot sticks and ranch dip.

Emma dug inside her bag. She had to take her stun gun out in order to reach her wallet that'd fallen to the bottom. She paid with cash.

The clerk, a young girl in her twenties fighting acne, didn't so much as flinch. The black and blue welt around her eye would've made that reaction hurt. Instead, she asked how much the weapon cost. Emma shared the price casually as if they were exchanging beauty tips.

"Would I need a permit to carry one of those?" the shy girl asked.

"For self defense," Izabella said, "no."

They found a clean table to occupy, and ate.

Emma chewed on small bites thoroughly, and filled Izabella in about finding another life model willing to fill in for her while she went to Norway; an exotic dancer who went by the stage name Trixie.

Izabella dipped a carrot stick in the creamy dressing. "Speaking of traveling, I saw the passport in your go-bag. I didn't know you'd ever journeyed anywhere outside the country."

"I haven't," Emma said, then washed some of her meal down with a swig of water. "It's just a contingency I keep on hand in case of an emergency."

●

The panel truck lumbered past old houses and historic structures that protruded from bluffs and lined the river. Izabella spun the big wheel to negotiate a wide turn onto Hilda Street. About half-a-mile up, the road lead into fifty-four acres of peaceful rolling hills. Established in 1854, Mountain Vista was one of the oldest cemeteries on the west coast. She stomped on the brakes in front of the Parks Department offices to the right.

Emma hopped out, the straps of her rucksack in hand.

"Thanks for the lift," she said.

"No problem," Izabella said. "See you soon."

As the utility vehicle drove off in search of a turnaround, Emma entered the main building.

"Good afternoon, Judy."

The receptionist looked up from the computer monitor. A purple wool turtleneck sweater kept the graceful and slender brunette's long neck warm. Dragonfly earrings dangled from her ears. The receptionist stopped typing and gave Emma a strained smile. If her kids grew up to dress like a glam punk, she'd disown them. Prejudice aside, Judy understood that Emma was entitled to pay her respects to the dead just like anyone else, so she treated her with at least a modicum of courtesy.

"Can I help you?" Judy said.

Sensing Judy's insincerity, Emma got right to the point.

"I'm looking for where Earl and Charlene Hellberg are buried, please," she said curtly.

Judy sighed, put out. She moved the mouse to minimize the file she'd been editing, then opened up the registry map. "They're interned in the southwest corner of section E along Brandt Lane. It's under an Elm tree. You can't miss it. Anything else?"

Emma walked away before losing her temper, or saying something that might get her banned from the property. She stayed to the left of the main drive and strolled passed the maintenance shed, over to section E. Judy hadn't mentioned that the Hellberg's tombstone was the biggest one in that row of the cemetery. A majestic angle of Mount Hood's snowy peak adorned the view.

The sun was beating down from a high arc, gleaming

light off the grave markers brightly. Emma stepped in the shade of an Elm tree. She smiled at Earl's and Charlene's names engraved on gold plates. Charlene had outlived Earl by four years. Death visited her three weeks ago, Halloween night, with a diabetic coma. She loved to hoard and sneak candy.

Her medical file enforced a non-resuscitate order.

Gratitude and regrets welled up inside Emma. Gingerly, she walked up to the stone, then knelt down. She placed one of the bouquets at the base, and tenderly caressed the top of the tombstone.

"Thanks for stopping that night," Emma said.

An unbeliever in prayer since the sexual assault, Emma took a few minutes to hold a brief conversation instead. She told the Hellbergs about becoming a forensic sketch artist. She complimented how beautiful their resting place looked. Their headstone must've cost a fortune, but with the Hellberg's hauling lumber and paper all up and down the coast for over forty years, they could obviously afford it.

"Excuse me . . ." a gruff voice interrupted.

Emma wiped a tear off her cheek and met the new groundskeeper. "Yeah."

"The souls here don't take kindly to strangers trampling over their graves," he said.

"I'm not a stranger," Emma said.

"I don't recall seeing you in attendance at Mrs. Hellberg's funeral."

One of Emma's day jobs had kept her from attending, and since Charlene wasn't a direct relative, funeral leave didn't cover a day off to go. If only she'd still been working for the county. Then she could've gone.

"I come here a lot to visit my stepmom," Emma told him. "Check with Judy. If you don't mind though, I'd like to finish paying my respects to the kind people that rescued me the night I was raped."

That shut the overzealous groundskeeper up. He left Emma alone. Still, she couldn't fault the guy for doing his job.

She shrugged her frustration off, and beamed her approval. "Good help here."

Emma said so long and promised the Hellbergs that she'd visit them again on their birthdays. She walked back out onto the lane, headed west, then turned north and ambled along the trees. The paved path sloped downward. A soccer mom pushing a stroller jogged by. Good workout for a mom losing her maternity weight. Emma heard the baby cooing and giggling.

Jenny was laid to rest in an older section. It was a stone's throw away from the property donated by the Masonic Lodge. Her father inherited the plot. His family had money. Their heritage went way back to one of the first timber industrialists and settlers in Oregon City.

He always hated that she'd married a cop from Portland. Nonetheless, Ted Cleveland let that sleeping dog lie, until his youngest daughter passed away. He owned the house where Glen and Jenny wasted so many dreams. They thought they were loving memories. Ted made the cop an offer he couldn't refuse.

Glen could keep the house and all the memories of Jenny there, but he had to allow Ted to bury her under the Cleveland name.

Emma sat down cross-legged at her stepmom's tombstone, a giant cross of granite. An intricate spider web clung to the open spaces between the top vertical and horizontal lines. The silk strands expanded and contracted in the wind like even breaths from strong lungs. Emma didn't touch it. She liked spiders. They were masters of geometry and perspective.

She brought Jenny up to speed about the events that'd happened over the last few days. After a while Emma stretched out on the grass. Her eyelids grew heavy. She imagined Jenny brushing her hair after the night terrors started. It relaxed her enough to doze off.

●

The minute Izabella turned back onto Molalla Avenue and trucked southwest, her smartphone beeped.

"Shit . . ." she said.

Taking a hand off the wheel, Izabella leaned forward and tapped the screen to silence the alarm. A pothole jarred the vehicle.

"*Shit!*"

She sucked in a quick breath of panic to purge the adrenaline that flooded her nerves, then put her hand back on the two a'clock position. Garlic, herbs, and pepperoni wafted up her nose. Just past a pizza joint at May Street, a handicap bus had pulled out right in front of her. Izabella tapped the brake pedal gently. The panel truck lurched forward to decelerate abruptly.

Driver's education shock movie footage of blood and guts splashing the windshield flashed inside her head. For a morbid second, Izabella wondered who would clean up after her when she bought it. At least she didn't skid and rear end them. She flipped a dreadlock out of her eyes.

"Come on, come on," Izabella complained. "Move it, assholes. You're going five miles under the speed limit. Christ on crutches."

The bus added two minutes to her three-minute destination time until it finally crawled into the parking lot for a retirement home.

Izabella hit the gas. She hung a tight right onto Warner Milne Road. A coffee cart she sped by was appropriately named Rush. Izabella signaled a left turn, veering into the center lane. After waiting for five motorists to coast by, she entered the northwest corner of the Hilltop Mall.

Specifically, the parking area for Oregon City Code Enforcement. The police station. Straight ahead, Izabella could see the gated entry to a secured lot. The suicide cleanup job likely awaited her in there. A chill enveloped her entire body. On account of how warm the afternoon had become, she couldn't discern where the creepy feeling originated from.

Izabella backed into a space in the southeast corner near. As she set the parking brake, Izabella eyeballed a man-sized hole in the fence line. She stepped down from the truck, and looked harder. The edges appeared to be melted.

She bounded up the platform of steps to the brown orifice, then pulled the glass door open. A hustle and bustle of activity swarmed the station. A blonde-haired bail bondsman with a teenager in custody was checking in his sidearm. The raised voice of a businessman disputing unpaid parking tickets and his BMW being locked with a tire claw boomed.

A few people gawked at Izabella's non-binary appearance and choices in clothes. Their gazes of disapproval ricocheted off her like bullets off a superhero. She understood that the average person in Oregon City was a little more conservative than a Portlander, but they needed to get over it. They acted as if they hadn't seen a punker before.

Izabella slouched an elbow and a hip against the front desk.

Sometime later, a balding, portly officer asked Izabella if he could help her. He earned extra points for not cringing or wincing at the multitude of piercings in her face.

"Izabella Sommer," she said in her gravelly voice, flipping her wallet open to flash her work I.D. "Aftermath

Cleaners. Apparently, you've got a car someone committed suicide in that needs cleaned."

"You're late," Officer Morgan said, then swung a visitor check-in log and a pen on a chain around for her to sign.

Izabella scribbled her autograph. "Yeah, made a slight detour to drop a friend off at the cemetery. Sorry."

"It's only a few minutes," Morgan said.

Then why are you busting my chops about it, asshole, Izabella thought.

She filled in her address and cell phone number.

"Are you carrying any weapons on you?"

"No."

He handed over a visitor's badge, then pressed a button recessed behind the counter. A door to the right of the desk buzzed and clicked. "Okay. Enter there and follow me. Stay close."

Izabella tailed the officer's massive back. The swollen bump below his thick neck was a prognosis for insulin resistance. He guided her through a bullpen of clacking keyboards and ringing phones. Muffled voices worked cases.

She kept her voice low. "I saw that your motor pool area had a recent break in."

Morgan's double chin looked over the shoulder of his ironed shirt. "Yes. Nothing was stolen, though. I don't understand why someone would break into an impound yard. They didn't even leave so much as a gang tag spray painted anywhere."

"My boss's text message about the job was sorta vague," Izabella said. "Can you tell me anything else about it?"

"A stripper shot herself in her car, a Honey yellow Camaro with black racing stripes. Beautiful ride. Custom engine. When I found that hole in the fence this morning I thought street racers had busted in to steal it. The department wants the interior spick-and-span so they can put the car up for auction on Black Friday."

The officer scored more points for holding the side door open for Izabella.

They walked toward the sports car isolated in a spot away from other vehicles. Half of the lot was empty with most of the black and whites out on patrol.

Officer Morgan pulled a set of keys out of his flabby pockets. He aimed the fob at the Camaro, pressed a button to deactivate the alarm. Two beeps blooped off-key. They sounded staticky.

Morgan stopped in his tracks. Izabella's shoulder nudged the officer. He gestured at the car with the fob again.

Beep-bloop.

The Camaro blew. An enormous red fireball mushroomed. Officer Morgan spun around, pale-faced, putting his back to the explosion and shielding Izabella. The concussive blast cracked or shattered every car window in the lot. The cop's body went as slack as a marionette with its strings cut. He fell on Izabella. She hit the ground and the wind in her lungs gushed from her lips in a scream.

A disorienting buzzing sound whined in her ears. Izabella grunted, mustering enough strength to push the fallen officer's dead weight off her boyish body. She felt hands latch onto her shoulders, dragging her away from the scene.

Izabella could barely keep her eyes open. She viewed the carnage through tendrils of dark smoke dissipating in the air. Shards of metal pierced Morgan's back. A custom license plate impaled his spine.

She mouthed the letters silently. "T-R-I-X-I-E."

The same name as the stripper interested in taking her place as a life model, and a witness Emma had been hired to interview for sketching a suspect profile.

"Emma . . ." Izabella murmured, then passed out.

●

A leaf blower was running nearby. Emma's cell phone in her jean shorts pocket began to vibrate. She raised her head up off her backpack. What really woke her up from a nap though was that same, faint curry smell.

Emma sat up on her knees and looked to the west. The sun would be setting in thirty minutes, maybe less. She wiped the sleep out of her eyes as they adjusted to the dusk light. After pulling her rucksack on over her shoulders, Emma dug the phone out and answered it. "What?"

"Emma, it's Heather. Where the hell are you?"

The despair in the detective's tone kept Emma from cracking wise.

"At Mount Vista Cemetery putting fresh flowers on my stepmom's grave. Why? What's—"

"Your sketch did it, Emma! Glen apprehended Bassim early this morning."

"Razor," Emma said. "Maybe we'll go watch one of those old movies to—"

"Shut the fuck up," Heather yelled, her voice tearing up. "And stop *interrupting* me. Glen's in the ER. He suffered a severe concussion from a blow to the head. He got the shit beat out of him, Emma."

On her feet now, Emma covered her mouth. Not only did the horrible news of Glen's hospitalization hit her where it hurt, the rank curry odor was getting stronger.

"Listen up," Heather continued. "There's more. You're in serious trouble, Emma. Bassim attacked his wife to prove how dangerous you are to his employers. His arrest this morning was set in motion to keep us occupied. We found surveillance pictures taken of you, Matt Grudge, Leslie Crow, and that stripper, Trixie, eating together at a—"

The groundskeeper turned the leaf blower on a few yards away. The loud lawnmower engine drowned out the last words of Heather's warning. Maybe the disturbance was his pathetic idea of forcing Emma to leave.

Spinning furiously on the groundskeeper, she shouted, "Turn that fucking thing off. I need to hear . . ."

The spices were too close and assaulted Emma's allergies. Dropping her phone, she bowed to sneeze.

At least the leaf blower stopped.

Emma stood up straight to thank the groundskeeper. Her jaw dropped. The guy crashed to his knees, a bullet hole smoldering in his chest. Another shot tapped his forehead. His blood pearled from the hole as he leaned forward and hit the grass with a final twitch.

Swiveling her head to the left where the gunshots came from, Emma identified her assassin.

The goddamn cook from the food trucks downtown stood beside an oak tree, aiming a suppressed Beretta right at her heart.

Dead leaves fell into his field of fire. Distracted, he pulled the trigger instead of squeezing it.

The shot sliced through the meat of Emma's right shoulder, spattering blood on Jenny's headstone. She clenched the flesh wound. Adrenaline fueling her survival, Emma sprinted uphill through the tombstones. Gunfire trailed after her, nicking markers or cutting divots in the grass behind her feet. Her red hair made for an easy target. So Emma weaved. She couldn't respect the graves right now unless she wanted to become a corpse beside them.

Emma bolted out onto the drive, then risked a look over her shoulder. The gunman crested the top of the hill too, leaping out onto the pavement, the tails of his untucked flannel shirt flapping. He fired a snapshot. Emma tucked her head in and forward rolled across the blacktop, skinning her knee to seek cover among the tombstones. She grimaced in pain and darted for the biggest marker along Brandt Lane.

Emma cowered behind the Hellberg's grave.

Unstrapping the rucksack from her shoulders, she flung it into the road.

Shit, I forgot to pull out the stun gun.

Emma thought of tempting the threat on her life by running out to get the bag.

Then the cook's voice called out, too damn close.

"Come on out, Emma. I promise to do you quick and neat. You'll still be able to have an open casket funeral. My method's a better way to die than Bassim planned. He wanted to strap you in a suicide vest and blow you to hell on First Thursday in the Pearl. A public execution to remind any other artist that might think of helping the police identify criminals. It's a dying art."

While the gunman monologued, Emma patted herself down for anything to use as a weapon. Maybe she could at least utilize her keys like crude brass knuckles. But they were clipped to the rucksack.

She found something.

Emma dug inside the inner pocket of her vest and withdrew a pencil. The one she'd used to draw the clue from her nightmare that morning.

She watched the side of the assassin's bald head appear. He walked right past her. Setting his sights on Emma's bag, the gunman began to turn his back. Slowly, Emma rose up from her hiding place.

The parking lot lights switched on and Emma's lithe shadow materialized.

Twirling around, the cook zeroed his aim. At 11pm, Emma kicked the gun out of his hand. The Beretta smacked the Hellberg's.

"All right," the cook said, "I'll take you hand-to-hand. By the time I'm finished beating your pretty face in though, you'll wish those rapists finished you off."

Her lip curled. "You've done your homework. Come on, dickhead."

Rage surged within Emma as she let the assassin get close enough to grab a fistful of her long red hair on the crown of her head. She ducked and weaved, dodging the punch he drove at her stomach. Emma's wig came off. The cook held the appliance in his hand, dumbfounded.

Emma jammed the pencil into his throat, puncturing the jugular, then yanked the sharp tip back out.

Blood spurted on his jaw and shoulder. He dropped the wig, then clutched at his throat with both hands to stop the bleeding, only the blood was too slippery. His fingers slipped all over his skin, unable to find the wound.

Thirty seconds later, the assassin was gurgling on his knees. His handsome eyes stared up at his prey in shock.

Emma simply stood back to watch.

EPILOGUE

Seventy-Two Hours Later

Four Polaris snowmobiles skied across the deep, vast snowy terrain. The riders stuck to trails marked by signs or tracks from other sledders. They wore heavy-duty boots, thick gloves, helmets, and snowmobile suits. The one-piece suits maximized insulation from the elements. No games. No "hot dogging," as the Norwegian outdoorsman in Alta that rented them the snow machines had put it. They'd all traveled a long way and just wanted to reach the cabin before dark.

Moderate speeds enabled the tight group all the time in the world to admire the majestic landscape. They spotted a herd of wild tundra reindeer.

The tallest rider in the back of the party kept a watchful eye on the side mirrors for any tails. Black skin scrunched up in the frosty air to stay alert and focused.

Thirty miles east of Alta, the sledders reached their destination inside a cluster of trees. Two feet of snow covered the roof of the secluded wood cabin. The lights on the snowmobiles shined on the icicles that grew on the bark of the trees, and weighted the thick branches down.

The shortest rider dismounted their sled. Trudging through the snow up to their knees in places, they made for a small tool shed beside the house. The rider returned with a snow shovel and cleared the front door alongside the cabin. While that task was being completed, the other riders dismounted, then unstrapped the bags on the back of their respective snowmobiles, getting ready to go inside where they could get warm.

After scraping most of the ice off the walkway, the short rider took one of their gloves off. The combination dial on the lockbox for the keys was small. Padded fingers couldn't turn it. Delicate, limber fingers spun the combo dial fast.

The sledders walked into their home for the winter, maybe the spring too, if the timeshare company would allow it.

Izabella, Amanda, Emma, and Naomie removed their helmets.

The women settled in. Izabella got a fire started. Amanda put her culinary education to use, cooking up a meal. Emma helped by putting away the groceries they'd brought with them from Alta. Izabella gave Naomie a thorough tour of the cabin, including a gun safe that contained a Glock and an old Winchester rifle. Two boxes of ammunition for each weapon were unopened.

A savory aroma of lemon-peppered salmon filled the cozy getaway. Amanda completed the meal with baked potatoes and a salad. Emma prepped the veggies. She got a few dicing tips from Amanda. She wielded a blade like it was a part of her hand.

At dinner, no one mentioned the deadly events that brought them to another country to hide out.

Emma and Naomie talked about it after midnight, while their generous hosts made love in their bedroom. Amanda screamed during orgasm.

Naomie toasted Emma with her mug of hot chocolate, spiked with peppermint schnapps. "Here's to love shacks and safe houses."

Emma clinked her cup of coffee against the mug. The pain meds Heather provided Emma for her gunshot wound restricted alcohol consumption. "To friendship."

"There's no way I was going to let my homegirl take her first trip abroad without me."

"What do you want to do tomorrow?" Emma said.

"After a hearty breakfast, I want to take a stroll of the perimeter in daylight. If an ambush ever comes, I wanna' know which direction it'll come at us from. Then, I want to check your dressing. How are you feeling anyway, sweetie? You didn't eat much of your dinner. Are you feeling feverish at all? Your pixie cut is starting to grow in nice around your ears."

"Thanks for that," Emma chuckled. "No, I'm fine. I just wish I'd received an update about Glen before we left the States."

"Heather seems like a straight up cop to me, and a protective guardian," Naomie said. "I bet she's watching over him right now, and she'll send you a telegram when his condition improves."

She'd have to. There was no cell phone coverage in their area.

"Hey," piped Naomie. "I think I saw some board games in the living room. Want to play Monopoly in Norwegian?"

"Sure, why not."

While Naomie set up the board on the dining room table, Emma went to their room. She retrieved a brand new tablet of drawing paper, a set of pencils, and a magazine from the nightstand between the pair of twin-sized beds, then returned to the kitchen.

As Naomie purchased every railroad her wheelbarrow landed on, Emma leafed through the latest issue of Italian *Vogue*. Emma's shoe went to jail. She didn't care.

Coverage of one of the biggest fashion shows in London made Emma use the bottom of a shot glass to enlarge a glossy photograph. She found the Grunge Operatives.

"Oh my God," Emma snickered. "Naomie, check this out."

She scooted over and looked through the glass. "Holy shit. Aren't they the private dicks you work with from time-to-time? What are they doing at a fashion show? Wow, they clean up nice."

Dressed in tuxedos, Matt and Leslie were standing in the back below the runway. Emma guessed they were providing security for someone. Maybe Leslie's friend that used to be a model before she briefly managed one of the food carts near their offices.

"Yes, they do," Emma agreed. "I just hope the trouble they stir up doesn't involve me again."

Naomie rolled double sixes.

They both forgot about the game to admire the northern lights that appeared through the bay window. The gorgeous ribbons undulated in a massive field of stars.

ACKNOWLEDGEMENTS

With special thanks to:

Ariel Hudnall, word wrangler and a friend who's always been supportive.

Jeanne Boylan's autobiography, for giving my imagination a spark that's been a constant star in my mind since the nineties.

Hal Harrison, whose professional courtesy pulled me into the world of photography. It encouraged me to produce and shoot the cover for this book.

Brianna LeBlanc for taking a chance on working with an amateur photographer, encouragement, and bringing Emma Rooney to life.

Crystal Laird for her makeup wizardry and backing me up when the groundskeeper mistook us for trespassers.

Melissa Kate, portraying The Muse in my new author photograph.

Angelique Herrington for shooting that photograph, and always being an inspiration of beauty, toughness, and survival that injects my women characters with verisimilitude.

The staff at Mt. View Cemetery in Oregon City for granting permission to shoot the cover there.

Tom Lupton for sharing a photograph of one of his subjects, which inspired the creation of one of the strongest supporting characters that I've ever written.

My wife, Kim, for believing in me, love, patience, and pulling me back from the dark places my writing leads me.

ABOUT THE AUTHOR

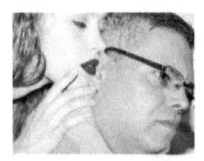

A Portland native, Aaron Hilton has worked at a video store, in a mail room, accounts payable, security, and for the last twenty years, as an alarm control operator for Fred Meyer and Kroger. He enjoys digital photography, film *noir*, pin-ups, scary movies, sequential art, and strong coffee.

He is currently working on the forthcoming titles in the Alternative Investigations series.

Photographer Credit: Angeligue Herrington